"Cold?" He raised his eyebrows.

"No, really, I'm okay."

She accidentally looked in the direction of the crime scene, and shivered again. Matt jogged to his car, retrieved a jacket and returned. Gemma thanked him and slid her arms into it, reminding her skittering heart that this wasn't high school, wearing his jacket didn't mean anything, and he was just being chivalrous—Southern, really—to make sure she wasn't cold.

"Ready now?"

Technically, she could only answer yes. Gemma had run out of reasons to delay this walk. So she nodded slowly, followed Matt as he started off down a path that she knew from experience would lead them from the clearing into a thick forest, dense with live oaks and Spanish moss whose shadows choked out the sunlight.

No, she wasn't ready. She never would be.

But someone was out there, someone who knew what she'd seen, and they wanted her dead. Sometimes people had to do things they weren't ready for.

So Gemma took a deep breath and stepped farther into the dark woods. Out of the light.

And back into the place that haunted her very worst dreams.

Sarah Varland lives near the mountains in Alaska where she loves writing, hiking, kayaking and spending time with her family. She's happily married to her college sweetheart, John, and the mom of two active and adorable boys, Joshua and Timothy, as well as another baby in heaven. Sarah has been writing almost since she could hold a pencil and especially loves writing romantic suspense, where she gets to combine her love for happily-ever-afters, inspired by her own, with her love for suspense, inspired by her dad, who has spent a career in law enforcement. You can find Sarah online through her blog, espressoinalatteworld.blogspot.com.

Books by Sarah Varland

Love Inspired Suspense

Treasure Point Secrets
Tundra Threat
Cold Case Witness

Visit the Author Profile page at Harlequin.com.

COLD CASE WITNESS

SARAH VARLAND

HARLEQUIN® LOVE INSPIRED® SUSPENSE

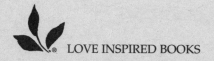 LOVE INSPIRED BOOKS

Recycling programs for this product may not exist in your area.

ISBN-13: 978-0-373-67759-7

Cold Case Witness

Copyright © 2016 by Sarah Varland

www.Harlequin.com

Printed in U.S.A.

But he said to me, My grace is sufficient for you,
for My power is made perfect in weakness.
Therefore I will boast all the more gladly of my weaknesses,
so that the power of Christ may rest upon me.
–2 Corinthians 12:9

To the women who have experienced pregnancy/infant loss, who know what it's like to feel as though that loss defines you at times. That's not how God sees you. He sees grace. He sees hope. He sees *you*. I pray for continued healing for all of us.

Acknowledgments

Thanks to my family for being encouraging, helping when you can, answering questions and all around being the best family anyone could ask for. I love and appreciate all of you.

Thanks also to my friends, both writing friends and "normal" friends. Your encouragement and friendship has been so important to me during the writing of this book. I can't thank you enough.

Thanks to Sarah, my agent. Working with you has been fun so far! I love that we are both juggling these jobs with the raising of little boys. Thanks for all you do.

Thanks to Elizabeth, wonderful editor and fabulous brainstormer. The work you have done already on this story has amazed me—thank you.

And thank You, Lord, for letting me tell stories and for teaching me things through them.

ONE

The steps groaned, the only sound in the south Georgia silence, as Gemma Phillips took another step toward the place she'd promised herself she'd never go again—the place where her nightmares had begun a decade before.

She took another step anyway, and another, until she was at the top of the stairs, hand poised to knock on the door of the portable office building where the Treasure Point Historical Society—and hopefully her future—awaited.

A month ago, Gemma would have said this job, helping the town develop and implement a marketing plan for the new museum being built on the Hamilton Estate, was beneath her. If she had her choice, she'd still be anywhere but here. But her job in Atlanta was gone and so were her savings. Treasure Point, where she could stay with her sister rent-free while job hunting, had looked like her only option—still did, unfortunately. And this job was the only one in town remotely close to what she enjoyed doing. She needed this to work.

But first, she needed to wow the historical society members. Surely after ten years, the cloud that had seemed to follow her, the looks people had given her, would have dissipated. Even small towns forgot eventually…

Gemma took a deep breath and knocked, shivering in the slight breeze that rustled the Spanish moss draped in the live oaks around her.

The door opened immediately, as though they'd been expecting her to arrive now. But Gemma knew without glancing at her watch that she was seven minutes early, just like she'd planned.

"It's you." An older woman gave her a disapproving stare. Not the first she'd gotten in this town, although she didn't feel she deserved them. Gemma'd been a straight-A student, always been nice to dogs and old ladies, and still, she was no stranger to that disapproval.

"Yes, ma'am. Were you expecting someone else?" *Right before a scheduled interview time?* Gemma added the last snarky question only to herself.

Cindy Anne didn't answer, only spun gracefully and walked into the office building.

Gemma shut the door behind herself and lifted a hand to wave at the other committee members, who were already seated at a long table on the far side of the one-room building. The man in the center didn't look familiar to her, but he stood and reached his hand out. "Jim Howard. We've spoken over email."

Gemma nodded. He was the director of the Treasure Point Historical Society, and the one who'd not only replied to her inquiry about the job but had treated her kindly with every response. Since he appeared to be the one in charge, maybe this would go well after all. "It's nice to meet you." She gave her best smile, tried to talk her shoulders into relaxing.

Gemma sat down, noting as she did that the metal folding chair sat directly in the line of sight of the window, in full view of dozens of tall oak trees, branches camouflaged by Spanish moss, where someone could be hiding.

Not that it mattered. She had nothing to worry about, not really. She was jumpy because she was back here on the Hamilton property for the first time in years, where her nightmare had both started and ended a decade before. Moments like this, when chills sneaked up her spine, were just aftershocks from those few months in high school when it had felt as if her whole world was being shaken. No one was after her now. No one needed to be. She was just ordinary. Normal.

"We're ready to begin." Jim gave her a small smile, which she tried to return. At least he was being kind, which was more than she could say for Cindy Anne.

Gemma sat up straighter, caught the window in her peripheral vision again and, again, tried to ignore it. She had to stop letting the past color every aspect of her future. It was time to prove to herself, to the town and most important to her parents, that she was more than the shy girl who in high school had testified at the trial of a smuggling ring and sent its members to jail. This job—marketing—was something she was good at. All she needed was a chance to make a good impression.

"Why don't you tell us a bit about your work history? Your résumé is impressive."

Gemma tried to keep her smile relaxed, but already she could feel her confidence building, excitement starting to buzz in her chest.

The next ten minutes were straight out of a best-case scenario. Everything pointed to Gemma getting this job.

And then Cindy Anne spoke up for the first time since she'd let Gemma in.

"And what about your past? To what degree do you believe it will negatively influence your attempts to bring positive publicity to the Treasure Point History Museum?"

Silence. Even the near-constant sound of bugs that Gemma associated with this part of Georgia was absent. Just this eerie, empty space where noise should be.

And for a moment, Gemma wanted to walk away. Let them—let the whole *town* think whatever they wanted. It shouldn't be this hard to interview for a job. She was qualified and capable. And her supposedly shocking past consisted of testifying against a bunch of criminals. She'd done the *right thing*. But for reasons she'd never been able to understand, she'd started being looked upon with suspicion ever since she'd discovered and helped break up a smuggling ring. If she could rewind the clock, go back to that night and unsee the crime, she would. Ten years later and she was still dealing with the fallout.

She made herself answer in a level voice. She'd faced people far more intimidating. But she'd never had so very much at stake. "I don't believe my past has anything to do with this job."

"Now, Cindy Anne…" another member spoke up. "I thought we'd agreed to give her a fair chance. She's the best qualified candidate."

Gemma wanted to let the words lift her spirits ever so slightly, but she was probably their *only* candidate. Not a lot of small-town people were drawn to marketing. It seemed for her whole childhood that everyone around here had a "what you see is what you get" view of life. And it wasn't that Gemma disagreed entirely with that perspective…but she'd always felt it was honest but still logical to be careful which side you presented, to let people see what you wanted them to see.

Around her, the committee argued. Gemma stared out the window, noticing someone walking near the edge of the woods.

He was a Treasure Point police officer, but he looked too young to have been on the force during the case in which Gemma had testified. Her shoulders relaxed some at that realization—she didn't have to hold against him the way some of the officers in that case had treated her.

The man came closer to the building, looked up at the window. Had he caught her staring?

Something about him was so familiar…

Then it hit her. Matt O'Dell, son of one of the men her testimony had sent to prison.

Their eyes met, just for a second. Gemma looked away.

If the Treasure Point Historical Society members hadn't forgotten her past, Matt surely wouldn't have. A shame, because he'd always intrigued her in high school. She'd always sort of wished…

"—trial period."

"Wait, what?" Gemma snapped her attention back to the committee members. She surveyed them one at a time, studied their faces. And didn't like what she saw.

This wasn't going to turn out the way she'd hoped.

"We think a trial period might be wise in this case."

Gemma shot a glare at Cindy Anne. The older woman lifted her nose and shook her head. "Don't look at me. I think hiring you at all is a mistake."

Gemma swallowed hard. A mistake? She pushed her chair back and stood. There was only so much she could take. If they weren't happy with her, fine, but she wasn't going to accept this kind of humiliation.

"Never mind," Gemma muttered.

"Wait," Jim called out.

She turned to face them one last time. She stared. Waited. They stared back.

"It's your choice," Jim said. "You can walk out of here with no job, walk away from this town again, even…but if you genuinely care about the museum, the way I believe you do, then you'll take the two-week trial period option."

One heartbeat. Then two. She let the silence stretch out, pretended to consider it. As though she had a logical choice. She was caught. And they knew it. She waited anyway, too prideful to seem *too* eager.

One more heartbeat.

"All ri—"

Her answer was cut off by screams.

In a man's voice they were even more terrible to Gemma's ears, especially because they echoed the screams she still believed she'd heard on this property ten years before—the screams the police told her she must have imagined, when she'd thought two of the men involved in the smuggling had started to fight.

One of them she hadn't been able to identify, though his voice had sounded familiar. One of them—Harris Walker, who had been somewhat of a drifter but had spent time in Treasure Point regularly—had been gone by the time the police arrived. No one had ever seen him again.

These screams were like his had been, and they took her back to those terrifying moments ten years earlier, when she'd been running through the woods as fast as she could, trying not to be the next victim...

Harris had disappeared and Gemma was almost certain he had been murdered, but no one had believed her when she'd told them. Not the police, not anyone.

After the screams came a silence. The kind that chilled a person to her core.

And Gemma knew her nightmare had come back to life.

In an instant, Matt O'Dell's patrol had gone from predictable to intense enough that he felt as if he was on the opening segment of a crime show on TV. He'd run from where he'd been patrolling in the woods when he'd heard the construction worker's yell. He'd found a group of them clustered at the outside edge of the construction site.

"What happened?" Matt directed the question to Ryan Townsend, the foreman.

The man looked up at Matt, looked back down at something on the ground and his face paled, contrasting starkly to his sunburned neck and shoulders. He shook his head. Not really an answer.

At that moment Jim Howard ran across the gravel parking lot toward the construction area. "What's going on?"

Matt saw several more of the historical society members clustered in the doorway of the portable office building. "Stop." He put one hand up and said the word firmly, shaking his head. "I need everyone back inside while I deal with this."

"But—" Jim started to argue.

"Inside, now."

The man turned around and went back, and he and the others went inside.

Matt approached the scene cautiously, trying to be ready for anything since no one seemed able to speak. The silence was startling after the constant noise of construction. "Move." The men stepped aside quickly. Not the way he had expected them to respond. Matt braced himself, wondering how bad it had to be to get a group of men like this to be quiet and compliant. They were nice enough guys, but they didn't typically like being told what to do.

He looked down at the ground, wet from last night's rain, and saw bones.

Hand and finger bones, reaching out from the dirt.

Matt felt goose bumps rise on his arms despite the eighty-degree heat. The bones seemed to be reaching up. Asking for help.

Treasure Point wasn't a perfect town—Matt had dealt with crime before as a police officer. But nothing like this. He took a step backward, needing the distance, and looked up to meet Ryan's eyes.

Matt took a deep breath and centered himself. "Tell me about how you found this."

Ryan's eyes swung to another man. "Bruce was working on leveling the site and doing some grading work. When he went on his break, I walked around a little, just to get a feel for the site. I do that with almost everything I build. I saw something sticking out of the ground over here, assumed it was a root and reached down to pull it up." Here he started to look green. "I looked closer at it and…" His gaze dropped down to the remains.

Matt looked down, too, then glanced up at the construction worker. Ryan's story made sense and it was hard to fake the level of uneasiness he was showing.

Someone had put that body in the ground, but Ryan was one person Matt was pretty comfortable ruling out, although he'd have to keep him on the official suspect list until he could investigate further. That was policy. Now he had an entire town full of people to consider. A whole state.

The bones looked old—old enough for the flesh to be gone—which made his chances of solving this case go down substantially. This was going to be like looking for a needle somewhere much bigger than a haystack.

The Treasure Point Police Department hadn't

had an official crime scene investigator until a year or so ago when Shiloh Evans—now Shiloh Evans Cole—had gotten certified and stopped working patrol to pursue her interest in forensics and crime scenes. A couple of the other officers could do the basic forensics work, and Matt could do it in a pinch, but Shiloh was the best. Assuming this was a crime scene, and not the accidental digging up of an Native burial ground, her opinion would be invaluable. And even if it did turn out to be an old burial ground with no crime to worry about, it was better to have been safe and called in Shiloh than to have compromised a possible crime scene and risked her wrath.

"I need everyone to move away from the scene."

Everyone complied quickly. Almost too quickly. Matt shrugged off the suspicion. The construction workers were spooked because they had discovered the body, nothing more. Their actions weren't indicative of any guilt. He placed the call to Shiloh, and then waited, standing guard over the body.

A police car pulled up only minutes later and Shiloh stepped out. She started surveying the scene even as she walked toward it; he could practically see the wheels in her mind turning, working at sorting out potential puzzle pieces. "What happened?"

"Ryan Townsend thought he saw a root and bent to pull it. Turned out to be a skeleton's finger."

Shiloh shook her head. "That'll give you nightmares."

"What are your thoughts?"

"You were right to call me. I think we're dealing with something more recent than anything Native American. This was really close to the original site of the Hamilton house, before it burned down last year. That place had been around forever. They would have known better than to build on any kind of graveyard or burial ground." She bent down, examined the bones a little more closely. "Besides, bone structure looks too big. We need to get an ME in here." Shiloh stood and shook her head. "I don't like how this feels."

Ryan walked back over before Matt could respond to Shiloh. "Do you need to talk to any of us anymore? Our shift's over, but we can stick around to give statements or anything you need."

Cooperative. That made his job easier. "It would help to talk to a couple people, but then you'll be free to go." As he gave his answer, movement near the portable office building caught his eye. A woman hurried down the stairs, and straight to the cleanest, most expensive-looking car in the small dirt clearing that had become a sort of parking lot when the Treasure Point Historical Society was meeting in their office. Matt frowned. Why was she running? He hadn't seen her at all today, so he knew she had nothing to do with the discovery of the body. In fact he didn't think he'd even seen her around town, although something about her looked familiar, reminded him of... He squinted as he thought.

Gemma Phillips.

What was she doing back in town?

Seeing her again here of all places messed with his mind. What were the chances? This was where the worst night of both of their lives had taken place—although Matt had had plenty of nights that were a close second with his upbringing. Though he'd always wished he could get to know her better in high school since she'd always seemed sweet and fun, they'd been in very different circles. And that night had driven the wedge between them even deeper, separating them further.

She'd left town right after they graduated, before he could ever work up the nerve to see if she might ever consider being friends with someone like him.

And here she was, turning up again when crime was surfacing in Treasure Point, which was a huge rarity. Did the woman just bring trouble with her?

Matt wasn't sure if she was leaving in such a hurry because she'd heard about the discovery of the body or if she was just anxious to get away from the place that must carry painful memories for her. Either made just as much sense. And either way, he'd put her on his list of people to talk to later. Something about the purposefulness of the way she ran... It seemed that Gemma Phillips had something to hide.

He just wondered whose life would be turned upside down by her latest revelation.

"I'm going to call the ME." Shiloh pulled her phone out.

Matt nodded, then walked in Gemma's direction. She was too fast for him; before he could do anything, even call out to her, she'd climbed into her car and driven away. He stood for a minute, watching her and trying to figure out how she played into this.

"You know her?" Shiloh's voice beside him caught him off guard. Apparently she'd finished her phone call. He nodded.

"Who is she?"

"Gemma Phillips."

"Phillips... Any relation to Claire at Kite

Tails and Coffee?" Shiloh's mention of Claire's coffee shop made him wish he'd swung by there on the way to work this morning. He'd had a cup at home, but the way this day was going, he'd need more soon.

"Her sister."

Shiloh's eyes narrowed. "Is she the one who testified in that criminal smuggling case a decade or so ago? She looks younger than I would have thought."

He nodded. "She was in high school at the time. How'd you know about that case?" Shiloh wasn't from Treasure Point originally, and it was a taboo enough subject that officers didn't even discuss it among themselves much.

"The smuggling ring was stealing historical artifacts. I found write-ups in old newspapers at the library when I was doing research for a history class I was teaching."

Matt forgot sometimes that she'd had a different life before joining the police department. It was hard to imagine her as a timid history professor. In his mind, she was 100 percent law enforcement.

"Why do you think she ran?" Shiloh was full of questions today.

"I don't know, but I'm planning to find out."

"Don't leave yet. I still need you here until

after the ME comes. This is your case, right? Your first big one?"

He nodded. His chance to prove himself as something more than a criminal's son, maybe the only chance he'd ever have.

Another police car pulled up. Lieutenant Rich Davies stepped out and strode in their direction, a determined look on his face. Next to him, it seemed like Shiloh stood up straighter. She'd had some unpleasant run-ins with Davies in the past. Matt felt his own shoulders tense. The way Davies was looking at him, he was afraid his time had probably come, too.

"You found a body?"

Matt jerked his head in the direction of the construction workers. "They did. I was patrolling."

"You can go back to it. I'll handle the investigation."

"I don't think so."

Davies said nothing but his face registered shock. More than anybody else, Matt did what he was told, took the jobs he was assigned without complaining. But after years of working easy patrols, of dealing with nothing more interesting than one incident of vandalism that had been tied to an adolescent dare, this was his chance to show the guys on the force that he was capable of real investigations, of doing something that mattered.

"We'll talk to the chief about this," Davies warned.

Matt only nodded. "Fine with me." The chief was a sensible man. There was no reason for this assignment to be taken from him—he hadn't even had the chance to mess anything up yet.

The chief pulled up in his own car and joined them moments later, ending their silent stand-off. "Officers, something wrong besides the body we should all be investigating?"

"I was just telling O'Dell that I was happy to take over the investigation from here." Lieutenant Davies spoke up first.

The chief glanced between both of them, settled his gaze on Matt. "Any reason you can't handle this case, O'Dell?"

"No, sir."

"Well, it's in your patrol area. I'd like you to see it through."

Matt blinked. Although he'd been hoping and expecting that he'd be able to keep the case, the relief of knowing his boss thought he was up to the challenge was so strong that he almost couldn't believe what he was hearing. He nodded anyway. "Yes, sir."

"Don't let me down. Now come on, both of you, show me the scene."

The three of them walked toward the remains together, Matt's head still spinning at the fact that he'd actually been given the case. He'd wanted a chance to prove himself? Here it was. Now he just had to do it—failing at this wasn't an option.

TWO

Gemma sat on her sister's porch swing, trying to enjoy the warm night, hoping the back and forth of the swing would calm her mind down enough that she could sleep. She'd run from the Hamilton Estate and come straight back to Claire's house, her home for now.

For a few hours, she'd debated her course of action—she could run and go back to Atlanta, find a job anywhere she could so she could at least live somewhere she loved…but she'd agreed to the trial period with the historical society, and she wasn't a quitter. Her only other options were to ignore everything that was happening and continue with her normal life—or to jump into the investigation fully and end this for good.

So far, she'd decided nothing. So she sat. Swinging.

Darkness fell faster than she'd expected— it always seemed to catch her off guard. Soon it was too dark for her to feel comfortable out in the open. Surely by now word had gotten around town that a body had been discovered. If it was tied to the crime she had witnessed all those years ago like she was almost sure of... was she in danger again?

Still?

Katydids chirped a night song, just another sound that was familiar and yet foreign to Gemma. She'd forgotten how loud it was even out here in the middle of nowhere. The sirens, the traffic she'd grown used to in Atlanta were absent, but the night noises were just as loud.

She'd loved this town once. Before its lack of support for her had broken her heart.

Gemma couldn't keep hoping this part of her life would go away with no action from her. She couldn't keep sticking her head in the sand, and she certainly couldn't run. Maybe going to Atlanta in the first place *had* been running, although of course her eighteen-year-old self hadn't seen it that way. But now, all these years later, it was time to face this. Past time. Gemma walked down the porch steps, climbed into her car, backed out and took a deep breath. She needed to go back to the office at the historical society.

If they were half the society they claimed to be, they'd have records. Maybe even records that might tell her more about the crime she'd uncovered ten years ago when she'd walked up on a gang of thieves hiding stolen artifacts deep in the woods behind the Hamilton House. Gemma wasn't sure yet what information about the items the thieves had stolen would do to help her, but she wanted all the information she could get. She'd never believed the case was fully solved. And the town couldn't move on until it was.

Neither could she.

Gemma swallowed hard, fought back emotion as she kept her eyes focused on the beam her headlights left on the road for her to follow into the darkness of the night. She'd run today because she already believed she knew who the body belonged to. And if she was right about who the body belonged to, then there was a good chance she was right about several other aspects of this case, too.

Meaning the Treasure Point Police Department had been wrong to declare the case closed.

Meaning that as Gemma had always feared… the man most responsible for the crimes still walked free. Maybe right here in this little town. And there was one more crime to add to his tally that she had been sure of—murder.

She turned into the Hamilton Estate, drove

her car to the construction site and parked but left the engine running. Was she sure about this?

It looked safe enough out there, although she knew looks could be deceiving. Gemma took a deep breath, shut off the car and opened the door. The minute she did so, an owl hooted. Startled, she slammed the door back shut, then laughed at her own cowardice. She was from here, not an out-of-towner. She should be used to those noises. Unafraid of them.

But the truth was that every heartbeat of the night, everything that should seem normal, took her back to that night when everything had started.

Being here again, seeing it at night, made her wonder if the setting would jog her memory in a way it hadn't when she'd been here in the daylight earlier, make her remember anything about the crime that had faded in her memory.

So far there was nothing new. Only fear. But growing within was also the determination to be done with this, to do something good for this town and make her parents proud.

Gemma *could* do this.

She opened the door again, this time squaring her shoulders and ignoring any odd sounds she heard. She walked across the parking lot to the building, pulling the key out of her pocket as she did so. They'd handed it to her just before she'd left that afternoon. It fit right into the door and she unlocked it, walked inside.

Locked the door tight behind her.

She exhaled deeply, shut her eyes and whispered a prayer of thanks that she'd made it this far. Gemma wasn't sure how God felt about her lately, with her losing her job, not attending church and all of that, but a prayer now and then couldn't hurt in her present situation.

Gemma clicked the light on, flooding the room with a warm glow that made her relax even more. The hard part was over. She'd made the walk from the car to here without incident—surely if someone had been waiting for her, they'd have attacked. She was unharmed, so it was likely she was in the clear. At least for now.

The office smelled musty, like a mix of pine straw, cardboard and something damp. It smelled perfectly like the history of the South. A small smile crossed her face. Working here wouldn't be so bad, especially if the committee members left her alone during the day and she got to immerse herself in other people's stories, learning about the past and doing something for the town without interacting with anyone else. It could turn out to be something she enjoyed, especially if it meant as much to Claire and her parents as she was hoping it would. More than anything, she wanted them to be proud of her.

"Okay, where to start first?" She said the words aloud to herself as she walked to the first filing cabinet she saw, deciding to start there, hoping that hearing her own voice would somehow make her feel less alone. At least when she was working here during the day she wouldn't be by herself. She'd be able to see the construction crew through the window. And even more interesting, Matt O'Dell would be here every day. Just as close physically as he'd been when they'd had almost all of their classes together their senior year of high school, and just as far away in every other way as he always had been.

If things were different between them, maybe she would have called him tonight. She trusted him more than she did any other officer at the TPPD. He hadn't been one of those who'd questioned her memories, who'd shrugged off her worries. After doing some research, she knew now that eyewitness testimony wasn't the ultimate form of evidence. If physical evidence contradicted it, it won every time. It was factual, unbiased. So part of the story she'd remembered had been ignored because nothing else had seemed to support it.

But tonight, she knew if she looked out the window toward the construction site, she'd see the crime scene tape from the scene they'd discovered earlier.

There seemed to be support for her memories now.

Gemma shuddered. It was time to delve into these files, the history of the town, and see if there was anything that could help her.

She searched through the green hanging folders, through weathered newspaper clippings and typewriter printed notes, for hours. She couldn't find anything that remotely tied to the case she'd been involved in.

Sighing, hating that she had to admit failure, she closed the file drawer and stood up, heading for the door. She slid her phone out of her pocket and glanced at it. Almost eleven—even later than she'd thought. Gemma stifled a yawn as she twisted the lock on the door to unlock it. The adrenaline and fear she'd felt when she'd first arrived had long since dissipated. Gemma reached to turn the door handle to open it.

It twisted. But the door didn't move.

Gemma frowned. She'd locked it when she'd come in. So turning it that way should have unlocked it…right?

She twisted the lock the other way. Tried the knob again.

Nothing.

Chills moved across her body. Sinister laugher

came from the other side of the door. Deep. Soulless. Gleeful.

Gemma swallowed hard against the pounding of her heart, which was pounding on the side of her throat, making it hard to breathe.

Relax. She had to relax. She took a deep breath, looked around the room. There had to be somewhere she could—

The lights went out.

Gemma dropped to the floor, crawled behind one of the desks almost without thinking. Survival instincts seemed to have taken over and all she knew was that someone was after her, very likely wanted her dead, and she was trapped in here. But she needed to keep it together, to stay calm and *think*.

Maybe someone only wanted to intimidate her.

The laughter came again, seeming to be the very sound of evil personified.

And then Gemma started to feel a touch of a headache, which spread quickly into an all-over ache, as if she'd come down with the flu in a matter of seconds. Was it fear messing with her? Or maybe the missing criminal had finally found a way to eliminate his last witness. A gas leak that could fill up the room with carbon monoxide would be an easy way to kill her and make it look accidental.

Her breaths were coming fast now from her fear, and she tried to slow them down, desperate to slow her inhalation of carbon monoxide. Did it work that way? If she tried hard enough, could she keep herself awake?

A window. She just needed to find a window, crack it open and maybe get a few breaths of fresh air. Her head hurt and her eyes, though she couldn't see in the dark, felt funny somehow.

Gemma pulled her phone out of her pocket, hesitated over the 9 that her fingers wanted to dial on gut instinct. Calling 9-1-1 would bring the Treasure Point police to her, but would they believe her this time anyway?

Matt O'Dell would believe her. She didn't know why she thought so, but she did.

She had his number in her phone, from when he'd called looking for her earlier in the day and left her a message telling her he needed to ask her some questions about what she might have seen. She'd ignored him.

She hit the send button, tried to put into words what she wanted to say to him.

But she didn't even get the chance to say "Help"—the only word she'd come up with so far. She'd only just dialed when her headache exploded.

And the black became blacker.

* * *

"Hello?"

Silence. Matt glanced down at his phone again, at the number he didn't recognize, though it did look familiar. It had an Atlanta area code.

Wait. It was Gemma's number. He'd called it earlier that day; that was why it looked familiar. "Hello?" he tried again, curious as to why she would be calling back at such a late hour.

No answer. He could hear background noise, although not enough to figure out where she was calling from or why. He'd expected getting hold of her would be challenging; was she really calling him back to talk about the case? Or could something be wrong?

He grabbed his keys, decided to try to find Gemma even though it was late. He'd head to her sister's house, where he'd heard she was staying, but first he'd swing by the Hamilton Estate, in case Gemma was working late there and had gotten into some kind of trouble.

The more seconds passed the more anxious he got. It was late—surely she wasn't calling to talk, especially since she wasn't talking at all. It was possible she'd accidentally sat on her phone or something and hadn't intended to call him at all, but she didn't seem like the sort to be careless in that way. Something felt…

off. And Matt didn't know why she'd call him if she was in trouble, but that was what this felt like to him. He tapped his fingers on the steering wheel, pressed the gas pedal a little harder. Two miles had never taken so long to drive. Matt drummed his thumbs on the wheel as he drove. He turned into the driveway and his headlights caught…

Another car. Hadn't he seen this one before? Gemma's.

Matt threw his patrol car into Park, opened the door and ran. He knew he was taking a chance of looking like an idiot if she was in there safe and sound and he was storming the place like this, but the lights were out. Why would her car be here if she didn't have the lights on in the office, working or something? There were no good reasons that he could think of.

"Gemma?" He reached for the doorknob. Locked. He fumbled for his key ring, hands shaking. They'd given him an extra key when he'd been assigned this patrol, since the Treasure Point Historical Society wanted everything well guarded but also didn't want the police to have to resort to damaging their building by breaking a door or a window. Matt knew because they'd told him so in a snooty way when they'd given him the key.

He shone his flashlight on the lock, shoved the key in, twisted.

He went light-headed almost instantly from the first whiff of propane. If Gemma was in here…

"Gemma!" He yelled it this time, no longer asking a question, but instead searching for her. Desperately. He reached for the light switch, but when he flipped it nothing happened. There went any hope this might have been an accident. Someone wanted her dead and Matt knew why.

You never could escape your past.

He searched for her, accidentally knocking into stacks of paper on the desk and hoping they weren't anything too important. Not that any pile of paper could be more important than Gemma. A mental picture of her teased the edges of his mind, her dark eyes wide. Vulnerable even though she had always been one of the most independent people he'd ever met.

"Be okay, Gemma." He dropped to his knees and felt around with his hands. The initial light-headedness he'd felt worsened. He stood, ran outside to breathe—through the door that he'd left propped open in the hopes of getting more oxygen into the room—and ran back in. "God, help." He prayed as he ran. Where would he go if he were Gemma?

Under the desk. If she'd realized someone was after her, she'd be hiding, right?

He stumbled to the desk, knowing if he didn't find her this time he was going to have to call dispatch and have them send the fire department, who had the equipment to do this kind of rescue.

His hand touched a shoe. Her foot. "Gemma?"

Still no answer. He removed his hand and felt along the floor about five feet. Her hand. That was what he'd been looking for. Matt moved his hands down the soft skin of her palm and felt for her wrist—and then her pulse. He breathed out a sigh of relief. Still alive. Matt gripped her upper arm with both hands, aware suddenly of how small she was, and pulled her toward him and into his arms. He inhaled and found the strength to stand. "Let him be gone, God. Whoever was here, please let him be gone."

With no choice but to pray and hope for the best, he ran out into the darkness, unable to reach his gun if he needed it since he needed both hands to carry Gemma. And leaving her while he checked the outside for possible danger wasn't an option—she needed fresh air if she was going to wake up…ever.

The darkness seemed thicker, more suffocating than it had when he'd arrived, even though the air was clean and fresh compared to the office. Matt took a deep breath, filling his own lungs with the outside air and then exhaling. He could only hope Gemma did the same. He laid her on the ground beside his police cruiser, deciding to give her one minute to wake up on her own before loading her in the car and driving straight to the small doctor's office in town.

It only took a minute before she started to cough, and sleepily sat up.

"You got my phone call."

Matt met her eyes and nodded.

Gemma nodded, too. "Thank you for coming." She closed her eyes again.

"Gemma, Gemma, wake up." Matt reached for her arm, helped her sit.

She did so, but she looked woozy to him, still.

"I'm taking you to the doctor."

"No." Gemma's protest was weak. Not that it would have mattered. Matt had already made up his mind about what needed to be done.

He drove to the doctor's office and at Gemma's insistence waited in the car while she went inside to get checked out. He was unsettled, antsy, but he couldn't very well go to the exam room with her anyway.

An hour later, she came back out. Matt got out of the car and opened the door for her, an action that was met with raised eyebrows. She'd been in the city too long. "How'd it go?" he asked as she climbed in.

Gemma shrugged. "Okay, I guess. He wanted to keep me overnight, but I told him I was fine."

"You're sure?"

The look she gave him before she pulled the door shut said enough.

Matt climbed in the driver's seat and shut the door, then turned to Gemma. "You're staying at your sister's place, right? Where does she live?"

Gemma shook her head. "I don't want to go home yet."

He raised his eyebrows.

"If I go home, I'll have to go to sleep. I'm not risking dreaming about tonight, not until I'm too tired to stand it. Is there somewhere we could go, just to talk about the case?" She looked away. "You know what, I shouldn't ask you that. It's okay, you can take me to Claire's."

"No, it's fine. We should discuss the case anyway. And I know where we can go."

"You're sure?"

Matt nodded.

"Could I borrow your phone real quick, to let my sister know where I'm going?"

He handed it to her, trying not to eavesdrop on the call—an impossible goal when he was sitting two feet away from her.

"Claire, it's me."

Matt couldn't make out the words on the other end of the line, but the tone sounded less than happy.

"I'm fine, I'm sorry… Yeah, I know you were worried. But I'm fine."

More words from Claire.

"I was doing some investigating and someone tried to kill me. I just finished at the doctor and I promise I'm fine. It's a long story… Yes, I promise I'm fine… Claire, really… Yes, I'm really okay, please calm down for now, okay?… Yes, they're looking for the guy. Listen, I don't want to go to sleep yet so I'm going to be with Matt for a little while… Yes, Matt O'Dell…I know. Okay… Mmm-hmm, I'll be home soon, an hour or so tops, okay?… Love you, too. Bye."

She handed the phone back to Matt. "You don't have siblings, do you?"

"No." Another thing he wished he could have changed about his childhood.

"I'm going to have a lot of explaining to do."

"Unit 807 to unit 225. Call my cell." Matt's radio crackled before he could reply.

He turned to Gemma. "Shiloh. I need to call and it's about the case so I'm going to talk outside. You'll be okay?"

"I'm good, Matt."

He stepped out of the car and walked maybe

ten feet away. Just enough to have privacy in the conversation and still be close to Gemma.

"Did you find anything to lead to a suspect?" he asked when she answered, unable to wait to hear what she'd discovered.

Instead, he got a couple seconds of silence. "Matt, there's no suspect because nothing appears different than it would from an accidental leak."

"What do you mean?" Matt glanced down at Gemma through the windows of the car. She was looking out the window, attempting to give him privacy, it seemed.

"There's no evidence, forensic or otherwise, that supports the idea of deliberate sabotage. We found a gas leak that the fire department is taking care of right now, but it looks accidental. And as for her being trapped... Maybe she locked herself in?"

"And couldn't figure out how to unlock the door?"

"Hey, don't get sassy. I'm just telling you what I found. I didn't say I was happy, either. Frankly, I'm not happy at all because this leaves me with too many questions and I was really looking forward to a good night of sleep tonight."

"Okay, you're right. That was out of line. But, Shiloh... She's not making it up."

"She's telling you the truth about what she *thinks* happened. I believe that." But Shiloh clearly didn't believe it had been an actual attack. And she seemed to think that he shouldn't have been so quick to believe it, either.

Had he lost all sense of his judgment at the sight of a pretty face? Matt was mostly sure the answer was no, but still, doubts haunted his mind. "I think she's telling me what really happened."

"Even though I have no evidence for you that backs that up?"

He hesitated. He didn't know Gemma, not really. And he knew and trusted Shiloh.

"I don't know." He let out a puff of air. Frustration, plain and simple.

"Just be careful, Matt. I know what this job means to you and I'm afraid that from what I've heard, Gemma doesn't exactly mix well with the Treasure Point Police Department. She may have helped with her testimony in that case, but it sounds as if she caused a lot of trouble, made them really work for the information they did get."

She'd been seventeen. Was he the only one who remembered that?

"Careful. I hear you," he promised Shiloh.

Matt hung up the phone and opened his door,

slid into the car. "Sorry, quick work call. I'm ready to go."

"No news, I'm guessing?"

Her brown eyes were hopeful. This wasn't the face of a woman who was lying. *Be careful...* Shiloh's warning faded in his mind the more he searched Gemma's gaze.

He shook his head, started driving in the direction of the Hamilton House. They'd swing by there, pick up Gemma's phone while officers were still there finishing their investigation. She could get her car another time, but Matt wasn't comfortable with her being alone in this condition. Then they'd head to his house. She'd wanted to go somewhere safe to talk, and that was the best place he could think of.

Deciding who to trust was a big part of his job. Matt could only hope he'd chosen wisely.

THREE

Inside Matt's house, Gemma could do nothing but stare. She'd expected that with a steady job and without his dad's alcohol habit, Matt would have a nicer place than he and his dad had had in high school, but she hadn't been expecting this. From the outside, it was a cedar cabin-like structure, two stories with a wide deck on the front. But the inside…

The front door opened into a living room with a ceiling that must have been close to twelve feet tall. She'd taken a deep breath when she'd walked in, exhaled and felt her shoulders relax almost unconsciously. The floor was knotty pine that was well polished and gorgeous, much like the stone counters that gleamed in the kitchen, which she could see from the living room.

"Everything okay?" Matt's gaze was amused, to say the least.

Flustered, she felt herself blush, but didn't know what to say.

"Hey, I was kidding, I'm sure it doesn't look like you pictured." Matt motioned to his living room couch that looked as though she could sink back in it and let all of her stress evaporate off her very tired shoulders. "Please, sit."

She eyed the couch again and took the big chair in the corner instead. She wasn't willing to let herself relax like that, not yet.

It was jarring to discover that she'd been right all along, ten years earlier. Someone else *had* been involved in the smuggling ring. Most likely had been the one in charge.

And he'd killed someone.

She swallowed hard, prayed she wouldn't have to run to the trash can at the revulsion that thought caused. Fear, terror, disgust… They knotted together inside.

"What do you know about the identity of the body they found today?" she asked Matt. Thinking of it clinically like this, detached as though she was part of the investigation, made her feel more in control.

Less afraid.

Matt shook his head. "Nothing for sure and nothing I could share anyway."

Gemma sat up straighter. "Why am I here,

then? You expect me to tell you something but you're not going to share information?"

"You're the one who wanted to come here."

She stood up, moved to the kitchen. "Because I knew you'd come ask me questions eventually anyway. I came tonight to get it over with." She heard her voice growing louder, but she didn't care. Maybe she was tired of dealing with all of this, maybe it was the lingering effect of the carbon monoxide or the treatment they'd given her at the doctor's office to counteract it—but she didn't want to answer his questions and then sit around and let a bunch of professionals with no personal stake in this sort it out. She wanted to be involved, to help.

"Then, let's talk."

"Not until you tell me what you know."

Matt was already shaking his head. "That's not how it works."

"Why?"

"You aren't law enforcement."

The quiet was complete enough that she could hear her heart pounding as she stared in Matt's direction. She'd hate to be on the receiving end of the glare she was giving him right now. "No."

His eyebrows rose, slowly. He was calm, in control, and it made her mad. "No?"

She folded her arms across her chest. "You

heard me." She shifted in the chair, managed to sit up *even* straighter.

"I'm a police officer and this is my investigation."

"And unless I'm being arrested for something I don't have to tell you anything. Isn't that right?"

Matt stared at her for a few seconds. Gemma braced herself. He'd always been one of those guys who was impossible to rile, who took everything in stride, but she was being enough of a pain right now that she knew it wouldn't be too long until he broke.

Instead, he just nodded.

"Then, I don't want to," she shot back.

"I guess I can see why you'd feel that way. I'm making coffee. Want some?"

His calm seemed to knock the fight out of her. Gemma nodded, felt her shoulders drop again. Coffee was always good.

The familiar sounds of coffee being ground—so he was a coffee snob, too; who would have thought the two of them would have *anything* in common—relaxed her somewhat. By the time he was pouring French pressed coffee for them in his straight out of *Southern Living* kitchen, she was downright comfortable. The tension had left her almost entirely and she was beginning to regret her outburst. Why did she have to be so forceful when she felt strongly about something? She had to learn to hold on to some of those emotions. It would pay off in the long run, especially while she was living this small-town life. Small towns tended to like sweet women. Not spunky ones with opinions.

She watched Matt as he worked, and found herself more fascinated with him than she should be. Everything about him was a contradiction, from the way he handled the French press so carefully while his arm muscles showed very well defined out of the bottom of his T-shirt sleeves, to the way he'd met her every argument and then let it go all in five minutes.

It made her want to trust him, something that made her stomach do flips—and not the cute kind you read about in novels. These were terrifying, anxious flips.

If the coffee didn't smell so good, she'd leave. The stress of the night, the overwhelming aroma of French roast coffee… It had gotten her to let her guard down, something she never did. No good could come from that.

Gemma stood to leave, good coffee or not. "I have to go," she announced abruptly as Matt entered the room, two mugs in his hands.

He just nodded slowly and reached to set the

coffee down on the counter. "I'll follow you back to your sister's."

No questions, no anger that she'd ruined what should have been a nice gesture, making the coffee.

Gemma hesitated, giving Matt just long enough to approach her. "Hey." He spoke softly.

Her face lifted to his, their eyes meeting. He hadn't touched her at all, but he may as well have from the way the air seemed practically charged with electricity. After just a second or two of silence that stretched out, he spoke. "You don't have to tell me anything. This isn't an interrogation, you aren't a suspect. Technically we have no links between this case and the one you were involved in, so you're not even a witness."

"Then, you wanted to question me because…?" she asked, even though she suspected the answer.

He met her eyes with an honesty she wasn't used to seeing, especially from people in her hometown. It seemed as if people preferred to keep their true feelings to themselves. But she saw no pretense in his eyes. Just full, clear blue.

"You know why. You of all people know why."

She did. Closure. Curiosity. That nagging,

haunting feeling that never fully let her rest, not even in sleep.

Gemma wanted to look away, but she couldn't. Not until she nodded slowly, admitted he was right. "Yeah, I know. But you also know why I want to leave the past alone. Let it go."

"It doesn't always stay there, you know."

As though she didn't. As though she hadn't had to fight for a job she was overqualified for because of the stigma of being involved in a criminal trial. "Listen, Matt…thanks for the coffee. But I don't want to talk about it. And if I'm not legally obligated, I won't. Not tonight."

"That's fine."

She hadn't expected him to agree immediately, with no fight at all.

"Stay anyway. Have coffee."

She studied him. Searched his eyes to see if he meant it.

Then Gemma sat back down.

Over a decade ago, he'd have given almost anything to have quiet Gemma Phillips give him half a minute's notice. Now here he was once again, unexplainably attracted to whatever it was he saw in her dark brown eyes.

She was the one to break the silence. "We

never talked in high school. Why are you being so nice to me now? When I…"

"What?" Matt asked, already knowing the answer. "You think I'd blame you for my dad going to jail?"

The look in her eyes confirmed he'd been right on. Matt shook his head. "He sent himself there. You didn't commit any crime, Gemma. You testified against one. There's a difference."

"Not to Treasure Point."

"Yeah, well, small towns." He shrugged. "But you don't really believe that you did anything wrong, do you?"

"Everyone treats me as if I may as well have been guilty. As if I'm a criminal by association."

Yeah, he knew that feeling.

"You don't believe that's who you are, do you?" Matt asked Gemma, feeling as though one day he was going to have to answer that same question for himself.

"Of course not."

"Okay, then, tell me about you."

"What do you mean?"

"What have you done since you left town?"

She eyed him suspiciously for a minute, as if she was trying to figure out his ulterior motive. He didn't have one, so he watched her back with a small amount of amusement until she'd apparently studied him long enough to decide he didn't have any particular reason for asking.

"I moved to Atlanta."

He laughed. "I knew that part. What happened between then and today?" He took a sip of coffee, looking as if he was waiting for her answer.

"Not a lot. I went to college in Atlanta, then started working at a company, doing marketing for them. They had to make cuts and let me go…but I know it'll work out."

"But you aren't happy to be here."

Gemma shrugged. Matt didn't miss the way she shifted in her seat, too. "I liked the city."

"Don't you like Treasure Point?"

"My family loves it and they're here. Family's important."

He saw her wince after that comment. Yeah, he was used to that, too. So he had no family, really, unless you counted his father in prison, which he didn't really anymore. Matt shook his head, tiring already of the conversational dance she was doing.

"Why won't you answer my questions?"

She looked in his eyes then, straight in. Something sparked in them that made him want to lean closer.

"I don't know why you want to know." Her voice was softer on the edges. Honest and unguarded.

"Because I want to get to know you."

Gemma looked away, shrugged. "There's not much to know, really."

"I don't think that's true."

She wouldn't look back at him. Seconds went by, maybe minutes. He heard her phone beep as a message came in, but she didn't reach for it and he didn't say anything.

More silence.

Finally Gemma looked back at him. "So tell me about you. Is this your first big case?"

Back to business. He guessed he shouldn't be surprised. "It's my first case like this, yes." He spoke the words to answer her question and also to remind himself. Putting aside a long list of other reasons he shouldn't be noticing now attractive she was. He needed to focus on work right now. Matt had wanted to be a police officer since the first day he remembered meeting one. He'd been five, maybe six, and an officer on patrol had found him up in a tree and bought him a Happy Meal when Matt had told him he didn't know where his parents were right then.

That was the day he'd decided what he wanted to do with the rest of his life; the day he'd decided what he needed to do to really *matter*. To be somebody.

"I saw more officers with you at the crime scene today."

So she'd noticed them as he'd seen her running away earlier in the day. Matt nodded.

"Did they find anything?"

"I thought we already talked about how you aren't law enforcement?"

She was the last civilian it would be appropriate to discuss this case with. It wasn't against department rules, specifically, to discuss cases, but officers were expected to use common sense and their training to make wise choices.

"It's late anyway." It was a lame excuse to get her out of his house, hopefully out of his head, but it was all he had.

Gemma's smile lifted slightly. "So you don't like to be on the other end of the questions. Interesting, I'll remember that."

The hint of teasing in her tone, the friendliness there, made it even harder not to trust her. Shouldn't he tell her what Shiloh had discovered, or rather, not discovered? Really, out of everyone she had the most right to know.

Then Matt pictured Lieutenant Davies, the smug smile that would be on the other man's face if the chief took this case from Matt and gave it to him. He couldn't let that happen, couldn't get stuck working patrol for the rest of his life. Matt was more than just a guy filling a uniform, driving a car with lights and sirens and making sure no one vandalized a construction site.

He was a cop down to his core. An investigator. Someone capable of helping bring justice when it mattered.

He just needed everyone else to see it, too, needed Treasure Point to see him for something other than his father's son. This was his only chance at proving himself.

And even though he'd been wrestling with attraction only minutes before, what Matt felt now was different. Beautiful as she was, all he could see in Gemma at this moment was her potential to destroy everything he'd worked for.

When he didn't respond to her, he saw her face fall slightly. With the night she'd had, he felt a hint of guilt for his sudden lack of friendliness, but he pushed it away. "I suppose you're right. I'm not big into questions." He made a show of glancing at his watch, not noticing what it said. "But it's getting late. You'd better head home."

She nodded. "Claire is probably worried even though I told her I was fine."

"Was that her who texted earlier?"

"I'm not sure. I didn't check." Gemma

slipped her phone out of her purse and read the message.

Then dropped it into her lap.

"Your sister? Everything okay?"

She just shook her head. He noticed her hands were shaking as she reached to pick the phone up, then handed it to him.

He took it from her, a frown already spreading across his own face. For someone who'd been so brave all day, the thought that a text could scare her this badly...

Then he read it.

He doesn't believe you. None of them do. I win.

FOUR

Gemma held her hands together in front of her, tight, wishing she had something else she could squeeze besides her own fingers.

How could he have gotten her cell phone number?

She glanced up at Matt, noting the tightness of his jaw. He was asking the same questions she was, but not out loud. Gemma almost wished she could talk to him, but...what had the message meant? He still didn't believe her?

She wanted to cry. Instead, she swallowed hard and made herself ask the only question that would fully form. "What now?"

"We investigate more thoroughly."

"Right. But I mean *now*. Am I in danger? Is he..." Her gaze moved toward the solid wood door. It looked secure, made her feel safely closed in from the night outside. But one good shot to the knob...

Matt was already pulling out his own phone.

It looked as if he had a plan. "I'm going to call Clay."

"Clay?"

"Officer Clay Hitchcock. We patrol together sometimes and he has a little fishing cabin near here where he spends all his free time. He can help me secure this area and make sure it's reasonably safe. Then we can get you home." He held the phone up to his ear and stepped away from Gemma. Her shoulders tensed. Being near Matt O'Dell made her feel safe. Who would have thought?

She wanted to let her mind go back to high school, think about the friendship she might have had with Matt if she'd been brave enough to strike up a conversation with someone so opposite of her, but she could think of nothing but the text message, and the impending sense of danger that pressed in on her like a tangible *thing*.

Gemma swallowed hard, feeling the beginnings of a panic attack. Was it too late to shake it? Maybe if she could have a change of scenery… Hands shaking, heart racing, Gemma wanted to run, but didn't know where she'd go. And it obviously wasn't safe for her, not anywhere.

Gemma swallowed hard, willed herself to take deeper breaths.

He doesn't believe you...

Did the killer know she was at his house? The first time she'd read the words, she'd assumed the attacker knew Matt was the officer on the case. Scary enough. But what if her stalker had actually followed her, knew where she was?

She sank a little deeper into the chair, as though somehow that could protect her from whatever evil might lurk outside in the darkness.

"I think he's just lent some credibility to your claim that this is all related to what happened ten years ago."

Matt's deep voice seemed deeper in the tension. Gemma turned to look at him. "What do you mean?"

"Until now, we just had suspicions. *You* may have believed someone was after you because of what happened back then, but it was hard to substantiate. His bragging about that, ironically enough, is what's going to make people believe you."

She narrowed her eyes in Matt's direction. "He was right?"

Their gaze had no sooner connected than Gemma jerked hers away, tried to school her features again. So she was hurt. Fine. She didn't have to show that to Matt, did she? Give him the power to hurt her more?

"Not what I meant."

"It's what you said."

Understanding dawned as she searched for some kind of indication that Matt was like the other officers, that he didn't believe her side of the story, either. She finally landed on it. Those minutes she'd been alone in the car, when he'd talked to Shiloh. His attitude toward her had changed after that. Shiloh must have told him something that made him doubt her story.

Just like the text had said.

Gemma did her best to leave her face expressionless, but somewhere in her heart, she could feel the battle going on between too many emotions to name. She couldn't let him see that.

She stood and walked away from him, momentarily forgetting her fear until she heard a car outside. Gemma jumped away from the window.

"Relax. It's probably Clay."

She nodded wordlessly and sat back down.

Matt reached to open the door. "We're going to have to talk about this later. About me believing you and about that look on your face."

He could read her so easily?

Matt didn't feel comfortable leaving Gemma alone, even for a few minutes. This case was growing messier by the minute, and it looked as though the star witness in the stolen antiques trial from a decade ago might be poised to become the only witness in a murder case.

Even if he didn't have a bit of a personal interest in her, her safety was too important to get sloppy about this.

So he stepped onto the front deck to meet Clay, leaving the door open six inches or so. He'd only be out here for a second.

"What's the emergency? You're going to have to connect some dots for me, man. I didn't go into work today."

"You heard about the body, though." Matt didn't doubt that for a second. First of all, Clay had law enforcement habits embedded too deep to have turned off the scanner all day, even for fishing. He was too protective of the town he was protecting during the hours he was on duty to ignore it just because he was off. Second, Treasure Point was a small town. Matt couldn't remember the last murder they'd had.

This would be news everywhere for a long time.

"Just that there was one. At the Hamilton place?"

Matt nodded.

"What is it about that place that attracts trouble?" Clay gave a fake shudder and Matt knew he was remembering a case they'd worked a year or so ago, one involving Shiloh and her past. They'd been present for the final showdown, which had taken place underground in a series of tunnels that led to the old house, and while everything had turned out well, it could have just as easily turned out ugly.

"It's in the woods, just out of town…" There were plenty of reasons the place seemed like a crime magnet.

"Yeah. Tell me about this one."

Matt shook his head. "I will. Inside. I have a…" What did he call her? She wasn't officially a witness yet. Saying he had a woman inside just sounded as though he had some kind of date, which hadn't been true for him in years. Women in his dating pool wanted to settle down, raise families, and no one wanted to consider doing that with a man whose dad was a felon.

"You have a what?"

Clay's gaze moved behind Matt and he turned slightly to see that Gemma had walked up behind him. He took in her appearance again, trying to see her through Clay's eyes. A dark purple fitted T-shirt that somehow managed to highlight the honey flecks in her brown eyes, and comfy sweatpants. Her dark hair was pulled back in a ponytail. She looked as if she'd put zero effort into her appearance, but she could draw the attention of anyone she wanted.

And the attention of those she wouldn't want, too. Like himself. Yeah, Matt was pretty sure he was down on the list pretty close to last as far as people she'd ever want to get involved with. No way she'd trust him after the way his family's past had affected hers.

And he didn't blame her. People could move on, but they couldn't erase things that had happened, could they?

"Matt?"

Clay's eyebrows were raised and the smirk on his face hinted that this might not have been the first time he'd called his name.

Oops.

"This is Gemma Phillips." Matt switched to his all-business police officer voice, introducing them since Clay had moved to town about a year after Gemma had graduated and move to Atlanta. Clay's amusement didn't dim at all. Yeah, his friend knew him too well for that.

"She has something to do with you calling me over here when I was fishing?"

Matt hesitated, not sure how to say it.

"Somebody's trying to kill me."

"You don't sugarcoat things, do you? Why don't y'all let me come inside so we can shut this door and talk…" Clay's voice trailed off.

Matt and Gemma stepped back almost in sync and Clay moved inside, toward the kitchen. Matt locked the door tightly behind him, still not sure what their best next step was. Were they being watched? Should he head outside to canvas the perimeter?

He looked over at Gemma again. She was a strong woman. He'd always thought so. But leaving her inside, even with a gun—provided she knew how to use one, as he suspected a Southern woman like her would—didn't feel like the right choice.

"The house is secure already?" Clay turned to Matt to confirm. Matt nodded.

"There doesn't seem to be an immediate threat," he admitted. "But someone is after her, and he seems to know she's here." He explained about the text message.

"Have you checked things out outside?"

He shook his head.

"He didn't want to leave me alone," Gemma chimed.

Okay, so she was more perceptive than he'd thought. There was a good chance he was underestimating her ability to handle the situation, but he wanted to take care of her. Was that so wrong?

"I'll take care of it. Tell me the rest of what's been going on. Start with the body."

Matt gave him the short version. Clay just kind of took it in, nodded and seemed to think about it without saying much.

Clay was steady, not quick to jump to conclusions. He could spring into action when he needed to on the job and react quickly, too, but if he had the choice, he'd take things slow.

The opposite of Matt.

"So far it hasn't been that bad, right? Besides the carbon monoxide thing?"

Matt raised his eyebrows at his friend. Seriously, had he been listening? "Isn't that bad enough? It could have killed her." The pale shade of Gemma's face seemed to imply that she agreed with him.

"Listen, though, he could have shot her, finished things quick and certain. With the gas, there was always a chance she could escape. What if it was a warning? Maybe he figured that if she didn't die, that would be enough to scare her off, especially when he followed it up with a text message and then coming over here."

"So you don't think it will get worse?"

Matt wasn't happy with the lilt of hope in Gemma's voice. He liked how it sounded, but it was false hope right now, and he couldn't let her hang on to it. "I don't think we can say that for sure." He glared at Clay with a "thanks a lot" kind of expression.

Gemma's shoulders fell. Matt noticed for the first time how much more exhausted she looked even than she had after the carbon monoxide incident earlier.

"All right, if that's all I need to know, I'll head out and check things out."

"Be careful," Gemma urged.

Clay smiled and nodded. "Yes, ma'am. I will be."

Matt followed him to the door, then locked it behind him after he left. He turned back to Gemma.

Matt's eyes on hers seemed to look deep into the tangle of fears weaving its way around her heart. His expression had become more serious since the text message. Even though he'd been so insistent earlier that he didn't want to push her into sharing more about the past than she was comfortable with, Gemma knew the rules had changed at this point. The text message had been a game changer, and everything was going to be different now.

Her heartbeat quickened and she had to remind herself to breathe deeply as she waited for what he'd say. She couldn't bring herself to just volunteer the information. She needed him to ask, needed to know that he wanted to be invited into the not-so-pretty sections of her past.

Another deep breath. And another. She wasn't ready.

"Do you have any more coffee?" she stalled.

"Gemma." He shook his head. "I'm pretty sure you don't need more coffee with whatever drugs you've got in your system that they gave you after the carbon monoxide."

Her shoulders slumped as he sat down on the other end of the couch and looked at her. "I know I told you we wouldn't talk about it..."

He trailed off. Gemma looked away.

Since she was looking at the wall, studying the mounted fish trophies that somehow looked not awful in this cabin, she didn't see Matt reach out.

But she sure felt his hand cover hers and squeeze.

She swung her head back around, eyes meeting his with no hesitation. She'd expected him to yank his hand away quickly, but he let it stay there.

"I want to keep you safe, but I don't know how to do that when I don't have the whole story. He's going to be one step ahead of me, Gemma, trying to get you, if I don't know at least what you do about who he could be."

This time the skipping of her heart had more

to do with the emotion in his words, the words themselves and how he cared, than with fear. Something deep inside her felt...something.

"And, Gemma, I'm willing for this to go both ways. You tell me what really happened that night, trust me with that, and I'll keep you in the loop on my investigation."

He didn't break eye contact as he said it. Everything about his body language backed up his words—he was telling the truth.

An inside look at the case, through his eyes? That would keep her close to it. Ensure that she could do everything possible to guarantee all the loose ends were tied up this time, that she really got closure and her life back.

Her *self* back. She was tired of being known as the girl who'd been through this or that related to the trial.

She wanted to just be Gemma Phillips.

Ending this case would let her do that, at least she hoped so. Which was why she nodded. Took a deep breath.

"You already know I was on a walk on the Hamilton property when I saw those men. I guess maybe I was curious, I don't know, but once I saw movement, I studied them for a minute while I was walking, just curious about what they were doing. They were burying things in the ground, which struck me as odd."

Matt nodded. "I remember this part. I paid attention at the trial—I knew you'd tell the truth about what really happened and I wanted to know."

"Really?" Gemma had known Matt was there, but had assumed that when she'd talked he'd probably tuned her out. It went right along with her assumption that he would probably always hate her for her part in putting his dad behind bars. Now he was telling her he'd listened? And…appreciated what she'd had to say?

When had she ever felt as if anyone had appreciated the sacrifices she'd made to testify?

"I always wanted to tell you," he admitted, his eyes not wavering from her.

Somehow it gave her the strength she needed to keep going. Gemma squeezed her eyes shut, then forced them back open. Stood up and started to pace.

"I saw them burying boxes. You heard all of that testimony, so there's no need to go over it again." Anytime anyone brought it up she saw the whole thing in her head all over again. Saw them behind the hanging Spanish moss, thinking no one saw or heard them as they talked about what they'd done, how many estates they'd stolen things from. She'd recognized a couple of them. Matt's dad, for one, and Rich

Thompson, who'd worked at a gas station not far out of town. Several of them were unfamiliar to her, but she could tell by their accents that they were mostly local. Not necessarily from Treasure Point, but at least from this corner of Georgia.

"I ran back toward the Hamilton House, but I tripped. The doctor told me later it was the worst ankle sprain he'd seen in his career. In any case, I fell." Hard. The pine straw on the forest floor must have muffled her fall. Either that or the men she'd seen next had been too distracted by their own disagreement to notice a little bit of noise in the woods...

Her own heartbeat had been the loudest thing in her ears then, even when the men's fighting had grown louder. They couldn't have been standing more than thirty feet from her, off the little game trail she'd been using. She'd only seen the other men a minute before—they were close enough that she assumed they were together, even before she heard what these men were saying.

"Gemma?"

She had to blink to see Matt and his living room, rather than the dark, thick Southern woods she'd been lost in, in her mind. When she finally focused she noticed she'd stopped pacing. She was standing in the middle of the room, suddenly afraid to go on, afraid to move.

Somehow afraid that someone was watching...

Listening?

"Gemma." Matt was up from his place on the couch now, moving toward her. All she could do was shake her head.

"What is it? You can trust me. You know that. I know you do."

He was right. She did trust him, for reasons she couldn't explain even if she tried. But she couldn't shake her sudden uneasiness.

What she was about to say she'd only said out loud a handful of times. Once the police had decided that this part of her testimony was questionable, that it had too many gaps to be useful, she'd stopped telling this half of her story.

"They were fighting." She lowered her voice. Looked around the room again. No one was eavesdropping. Gemma tried to use logic to calm her fears. Matt was inside and hadn't noticed anything else unusual since the text message, and Clay Hitchcock was out there somewhere in the night.

No one else was here. She took a deep breath. Time to be brave whether the emotions were there or not. "They were fighting and I interrupted them. Harris Walker is the only one I could identify for sure. The other man had his back to me. His voice sounded familiar, but I never could place it."

"That's not uncommon in situations like these. Sometimes the trauma makes it too much for the brain to process."

Gemma nodded. That was what she had assumed. "Anyway, when I fell, my ankle hurt too much for me to move right away, and I could hear them talking. Their voices were tense and it wasn't long before their fight got out of hand. Harris wanted more money—I assume from his part in stealing the antiques I'd seen the other men hiding—and the other man wouldn't give it to him. The argument grew more heated. The last thing I heard was Harris threatening the other man. Even though my ankle felt as if it was on fire, I got up and ran anyway. I was afraid that if they saw me, they'd kill me. All I could hear from then on was my heartbeat and the pounding of my feet as I ran. I don't know if he was shot or killed some other way, I just know that no one ever saw him again. And I think I was yards away when he was murdered, the second-to-last person to see him alive."

Matt sat silently for a minute, nodding as he studied her face, looking like he was absorbing her story, taking it in. "And no one believed you?"

"No." Gemma tried to keep the bitterness out of the word, but it was a struggle. Ten years later and she was still paying the price for everyone's distrust of what she'd been so sure she'd seen. Although she would admit that by the time the case had gone to trial, so many people had tried to convince her that she'd been mistaken that she'd started to doubt a little herself.

But they were her memories. She never had doubted them fully. Just pushed them away, tried not to think about them.

A lot of good that had done.

"So you believe the body they found today is Harris Walker's. He didn't live here, did he? I know I only saw him in town some, though I think he was one of the guys my dad drank with at the bar."

"I don't know where he lived, but I always thought of him as a drifter."

"So no family. That's why no one looked too hard when he disappeared."

True, sadly.

"So we have a place to start. Your memories, my current investigation." Matt took a breath, let it out. "I think we can do this, Gemma."

"I need you to *know* that we can."

He nodded. "All right. I know we can. Let me take you back to Claire's. Try to get some sleep. I'll come back here and do the same, and we'll get together as early as we can tomorrow to figure out where to go from here. The department won't put security on you since they don't fully believe your story. One text message won't be enough to convince them, but I believe the threat is real, and I won't let anything happen to you. I'll stick close—you have my word."

It was the best thing Gemma had heard all night. She smiled at him, nodded and followed him to the car.

When she got home Claire was awake, even though she'd have to get to her coffee shop around four or five in the morning to do the baking for the day. "I'm sorry, Claire. I forgot you would wait up."

Claire pulled her fuzzy pink bathrobe tighter around her, stifled a yawn. "It's okay. I just wanted to see that you were home and really safe. Tell me again what happened—I heard something about someone finding a body out at the Hamilton place? Were you there interviewing for the job when that happened?"

"Yeah." Gemma didn't have the strength to rehash everything again tonight, but she understood why her sister wanted to know. She cared, and that was nice. The two of them had always been close, from the day Gemma had been adopted as a four-year-old and become part of six-year-old Claire's family. So Claire deserved at least some answers now, no matter how late it was. "The short version is…remember when I said I saw Harris Walker at the Hamilton property years ago, on the night of that robbery?"

"Yeah."

"Well, I'm pretty sure it's his body that was found today. And I'm pretty sure that I'm the only one who might be able to identify the man who killed him."

Claire looked fully awake now. "What?"

"I know. It's bad. But Matt is going to solve it." She really believed that. The determination she'd seen on his face tonight… She wanted to believe it was all about keeping her safe, but Gemma knew full well he had a stake in seeing this case finished for good, as well. Either way, he had more than enough motivation and she thought he seemed like someone who was a good investigator.

"Matt O'Dell?"

"I don't want to hear it tonight." Another part of being sisters. They could just as quickly irritate each other as support each other. Matt had been her security tonight, believed her when no one else in the police department had. She trusted him in return.

"Don't let him hurt you, Gemma. If he makes you cry…"

Her sister may have been the epitome of sweetness, spice and everything nice, but Gemma knew she'd always fight for those she loved. "It's not like that, Claire. And anyway, it's time for bed."

"All right, I'll drop it for now. Only because you're right, we need to sleep."

The sisters hugged good-night and went to their respective rooms. Gemma double-checked her window to make sure it was locked, then lay down in bed, sure that sleep would never come. But sometime in the darkness, she thought about Matt, of the way he'd treated her tonight, the amount of kindness he'd shown her.

And somehow the bad dreams were chased away before they could even show up, and Gemma fell asleep in no time at all.

FIVE

Night had barely faded into daylight in the sky when Matt pulled his patrol car in at the Hamilton Estate. He and Shiloh were supposed to meet with a forensic specialist from Savannah at eight that morning, which was another couple hours away, but it didn't surprise him that Shiloh's car was in the lot already, too.

He put the car in Park, grabbed the thermos of coffee he'd brought and climbed out. He could see Shiloh kneeling in the dirt next to where the body had been discovered. He headed her way, taking a sip of coffee as he did so. The way the week was going he was going to need all the caffeine he could get and more just to keep a clear head. This body... It was likely the first murder victim in years for Treasure Point. This case was going to be a mess even without the added complication of the danger it brought to Gemma.

If he could separate the two of them, forget

about Gemma and his past attraction to her, he would. Unfortunately for both of them, it was looking as though she was tied to this case tighter than either of them would have wished.

"What do you think?" Matt asked Shiloh as he approached.

She looked up at him, a frown on her face. She shook her head. "I don't like it. This section of forensic anthropology isn't my specialty, but I don't think this guy got here naturally."

"Since people don't generally get buried three feet underground naturally..." Matt drawled the words slower than usual.

Shiloh's frown switched to a glare. "You know what I mean."

"You think the guy was murdered, and the killer buried him here. I agree."

She studied him for a minute. Matt looked away, not sure how much of Gemma's story he should share. On one hand, it sounded as though some of the officers involved hadn't handled her testimony well years ago, so he understood why she was hesitant to tell the entire department. But this was Shiloh. Matt trusted her, knew that Gemma could, too. But maybe that should be Gemma's decision to make?

Shiloh looked away before he'd decided whether or not he should share what he knew.

"So is she coming back today, or did yesterday scare her right out of town?"

"Who?" When Shiloh started asking questions, she got downright inquisitive in a ridiculous big-sister kind of way. He had to stop this as soon as he could or he'd be confessing his ancient crush on Gemma and all kinds of silly things.

"The woman who was here yesterday? The one you couldn't stop staring at?"

"Maybe I was keeping my eyes on a woman who could have a tie to this case?"

Shiloh shook her head before she stood and walked back to her car to retrieve something. "Not how you looked at her," she called back, her voice raised.

The crunch of another car's tires coming down the drive caught their attention and Matt swiveled his gaze in that direction.

Gemma. It shouldn't surprise him that she was here early this morning, either, he supposed.

Shiloh had looked back down to continue rummaging through her car, but looked back up when Gemma opened her door. "Hey. I'm Shiloh Evans Cole, Treasure Point Police Department."

"Gemma Phillips." If she was nervous as she stuck her hand out to shake Shiloh's, Matt saw none of it. In fact, he saw very little of the Gemma he'd seen last night—this one was all city clothes and confidence, from her glossy, straightened hair to the toes of her dark high heels. A far cry from her ponytail and sweat-pants.

It only took him about half a second to decide he liked both versions.

"You're new here, right?"

Gemma shook her head. "Well, new and old. I'm from here originally, but had been in Atlanta until recently. Now I'm back…"

Her voice trailed off and a hint of insecurity returned as her gaze moved to where the body had been found—where it still lay mostly buried in the hard, plaster-like Georgia clay.

"Not a very nice welcome. No one would like this being their first experience when they're back in town."

Shiloh was digging now. He wasn't going to let her try to get information out of Gemma, not like this. He stepped forward, closer to where they were talking, and interrupted before Gemma could respond. "Not a good welcome at all. But we're going to do what we can do make this—" Matt motioned to the crime scene tape "—all go away so you can focus on whatever you're doing for the historical society. You got a job with them, right?" He thought she'd mentioned something about that yesterday, though he'd been more focused on what she had to say that was related to the case.

"Yes, it's a marketing job."

"Have you met Mary Hamilton yet, the woman who owns all this and gave the town this little section of land to use for the museum? Or did you know her when you were in town before?" Shiloh grinned. "She's one of my favorite people here."

Matt laughed. "Yeah, well, she wasn't anyone's favorite a few years ago when she was driving all of us at the station crazy with those calls about nothing."

Shiloh looked at Gemma, eyebrows raised. "Spoiler alert—turned out she had a reason for the calls. They weren't about nothing after all. Now that I know that, she's actually kind of an interesting woman."

"She's not boring, that's for sure." The last time Matt had seen her, she'd asked him why he wasn't married yet and then started in with a list of her friends' granddaughters that she should set him up with.

"I haven't spoken to her yet since I've been back." Her look changed a little. Matt could only describe it as a "work face." She looked pensive and creative at the same time, as if the question had triggered an idea for her. "I should put her down on my list of people to talk to about the museum. I want to talk to some of the residents of the town, even ones who don't have much involvement with the historical society, to see what their vision of this place is. I think if I do that, I'll be better able to market it to them as something they'll be interested in. I'm most concerned with making the town fall in love with the idea of this museum. If the town loves it, visitors will, too."

"You think so?" Gemma talked about the museum as though it was a viable project. Matt had been assuming that it wouldn't draw much interest.

She looked offended at his skepticism. "Of course. In order for anything to succeed, people have to believe in it."

"She's not wrong, Matt," Shiloh seconded.

Another car approached the office building, and Gemma frowned. "And it's true for people, too," Gemma added. A man exited the car. Matt recognized him as one of the head honchos of the historical society. Gemma swallowed hard and said the next words so softly he almost didn't hear them. "And then sometimes, people have to do the best they can whether anyone else believes in them or not."

* * *

Gemma excused herself from Shiloh and Matt and went to meet Jim Howard.

"Good morning, Gemma." Jim was paler than he had been yesterday. Or maybe it was the morning light.

"Are you feeling okay?"

"It's this…this…discovery." He shook his head. Swallowed hard. He glanced at Shiloh and Matt, both in uniform. "But let's talk inside."

This sounded bad.

She followed him up the stairs, shivering only slightly as they entered the building where she'd almost died less than twelve hours before. Matt had explained to her that the police and fire department had cleared the building and repaired the leak, so it was safe to be inside. They hadn't found any evidence of the leak being intentional, though. Gemma didn't understand how it was possible—she knew what had happened—but she believed their assessment that it wasn't dangerous anymore. Still, it was hard to convince her feet to follow Jim's up the stairs.

"Mr. Howard, before you start—" Gemma started talking as soon as they were inside, before he'd managed to shut the door behind them "—thank you for giving me a chance. I know that some…some of the others didn't want to and I appreciate that you did."

"Yes, well, don't thank me yet. What did we decide? Two weeks?"

Two weeks. Hardly enough time to prove anything to them, much less to the rest of the town. Gemma nodded.

"All right, then, do the best you can. I have to tell you, though, after the discovery yesterday I don't have very high hopes for the museum's success."

That was probably the last thing she'd expected to hear him say. Gemma blinked a few times, tried to process his words and wished she'd stopped by her sister's shop that morning for coffee. "You've given up on it already?" She didn't bother to filter her words and make them sound polite—not if he was admitting such dire hopes for this project before she'd even been given a chance. Gemma couldn't decide which one she was more offended for—herself, or for this house and future museum that deserved a chance. The Hamilton House had always been a grand structure that reminded the people of Treasure Point of the past, both good and bad, and it was part of what made them special. Sure, other towns around had their historical claims to fame. Savannah was less than an hour away and had history coming out of its ears, but the Hamilton House had links to so many different time periods that it was still unique. Even though the original house had burned down, there was still something special about a replica of it being rebuilt on almost the same spot for the museum. It was almost like the grand old house could have a new lease on life…if they'd let it.

"I haven't…given up…" His words came too late, too slowly. Gemma was already shaking her head.

"This isn't fair."

This time it was his turn to blink back surprise. "What do you mean? Fair?"

"You hired *me* to take care of the marketing and publicity for the museum. I understand the discovery of the body…changed some things." Shivers crept over her arms. She definitely understood all that the body changed. "But the museum is still a viable project and I'm not going to pour my life into it for the next two weeks if you've already closed it down and packed up shop in your mind. I won't do it." Gemma shook her head, opened her mouth one more time as words she hadn't even realized she meant spilled out. "I care too much."

She shivered again, this time not from fear. She did. She cared about this museum, about this town.

It wasn't just about proving herself. She wouldn't, couldn't let the town down.

"All right, then…I suppose you do deserve a real chance." Jim's shoulders fell a little. "I want the museum to succeed. I just don't see how we can overcome something like this, get people to think about the museum without thinking about *that*." He motioned out the window to the crime scene.

She knew what he meant. Knew it all too well.

He didn't spend any more time in the office building, just left after pointing out a few things to her that she'd already discovered the night before—the location of the computer, the files, et cetera. Then she was alone.

Gemma let herself look around, absorb that she was really back here, for the first time since she'd walked back in. She could almost feel the heaviness in the air inside the building, weighty with the knowledge that someone had almost died here. That *she* had almost died here.

She swallowed hard. She had to get out of here.

Gemma ran to the door, shoved it open, almost expecting to be trapped again. Of course it flung open without a problem.

Matt looked up from where he'd been kneeling with Shiloh and someone else, working to exhume the remains. Gemma looked away, hesitated for a minute, then walked back inside, propping the door open with a portable file box. She was a grown woman. She should be able to sit inside a little building without incident.

"Knock, knock." Matt's familiar voice came from the doorway.

Seeing Matt lean into the room, blond hair messy from the morning breeze, wasn't an unwelcome sight.

Clearly her mind was still fuzzy from the early morning and yesterday's late night, if she was suddenly thinking it was okay to think of Matt O'Dell that way. He was the last man in the world, just about, that was appropriate to be seeing in *that* way. Surely he'd think the same about her.

"Hey," she answered quietly, attempting a small smile.

"Are you busy? I thought I'd see if you wanted to take a walk."

Was she busy? Well, since it seemed saving the museum rested solely on her shoulders...

Matt laughed, Gemma guessed at her expression. "I know you're busy. I meant, are you doing anything specifically or do you want a tour? I figured you should see the whole place before you come up with plans for whatever you're supposed to be doing. I didn't notice you seeing everything the other day before the body was discovered, and I know you didn't stick around long after, so…"

"That would be great." He was right. She needed to see all of the property near the house again, refresh her memory, not just for the museum's sake, but so she could help the police with this case if she needed to. Just because they hadn't needed that part of her testimony years ago didn't mean they wouldn't need it now. She'd rather walk around with Matt and dredge up those memories than do it by herself.

Not that she was eager to revisit those memories. She shivered, tried to rub the goose bumps off her arms before Matt noticed.

"Cold?" He raised his eyebrows. "I've got an old department windbreaker in my car if you need something."

"No, really, I'm okay." Of course, in trying to avoid eye contact with Matt, she accidently looked in the direction of the crime scene again, and shivered again. Matt jogged to his car, retrieved the jacket and returned. Gemma thanked him and slid her arms into the sleeves, reminding her skittering heart that this wasn't high school, wearing his jacket didn't mean anything and he was just being chivalrous—Southern, really—to make sure she wasn't cold.

"Ready now?"

She could only answer yes. Gemma had run out of reasons to delay this walk. So she nodded slowly, followed Matt as he started off down a path that she knew from experience would lead them from the clearing into a thick forest, dense with live oaks and Spanish moss whose shadows choked out the sunlight.

No, she wasn't ready. She never would be.

But someone was out there, someone who knew what she'd seen, and they wanted her dead. Sometimes people had to do things they weren't ready for.

So Gemma took a deep breath and stepped farther into the dark woods. Out of the light.

And back into the place that haunted her very worst dreams.

SIX

If Matt had thought Gemma was tense back at the construction site, he knew now that had only been a shadow of the tension that could overtake her. A glance at the tightness in her shoulders told him that this walk was costing her.

So why had she said yes?

He already knew the answer. It was the kind of person Gemma was—a quiet but implacable kind of stubborn. Now that she was back in Treasure Point and the case was no longer part of her past…she wouldn't disappear again. She'd follow through, finish this thing out, no matter what it cost.

Something that made him admire her and be terrified for her.

He turned to make sure she was still following him. Their eyes met and she gave him the smallest smile.

That kind of bravery may not look like much to most people. But Matt thought it was…

Beautiful. Like Gemma.

He shook his head, hopefully dislodging the thoughts. This was worse than the time in high school PE that he'd let a volleyball slam straight into the side of his face because he'd gotten distracted watching Gemma. Something about the woman had always turned him into mush.

Something he couldn't afford at the moment, not if he wanted to do the best he could at his job. *Keep* his job out of Lieutenant Davies's greedy hands.

Gemma's hand on his arm brought Matt's thoughts just as quickly back to her. She pulled him to a stop, turned him to face her.

"Wait." Her brown eyes searched his, desperate for something. Matt swallowed hard.

He wasn't moving, was he?

"We need to talk."

Matt nodded slowly. The case? Please let it be about the case, not about this chemistry, tension, whatever it was between them that made being alone in the dim woods with her about the dumbest place he could be. He wasn't sure he could trust himself not to act out the desire to kiss her that he'd constantly fought—and buried—years ago. "Okay."

"I don't know where to start. On this case, I

mean. I tried last night, when I was in the office. I was looking for records, anything that would help. But I'm a marketing specialist. I don't know where to start on this in real life, since my investigation experience is limited to late-night viewings of *NCIS*. I've got the memories…but you've got the experience with cases like this. So tell me. What next? What are we doing?"

It *was* the case she wanted to discuss. He exhaled, relief invading him. Somehow he knew kissing Gemma right now would ruin everything between them—destroy their new friendship, as cheesy as that sounded—and that was the last thing he wanted.

Well, second-to-last thing. The *last* thing he wanted was for both of them to end up dead because they'd let their personal feelings distract them from the investigation.

"Well…" Matt looked around. It seemed like an odd place for strategizing. Gut instinct said this stretch of woods had too many places to hide, too many places where someone could be listening.

So he shook his head. "Come with me. I don't want to talk right here."

Her eyes widened, fear flashing in their dark depths as understanding hit. She nodded. "Let's go."

This time he reached for her hand. He didn't mean anything by it, just wanted to reassure her that he was here, that he wasn't going to let anything happen to her.

But when she squeezed back and smiled...

Matt picked up his pace, and had to let go of Gemma's hand when the trees got too thick for the two of them to pass on the path together. Finally the trees started to become more spaced out, the woods opened up to a private stretch of beach at the back of the Hamilton property.

Gemma frowned. "I thought we were looking around the property. This is the beach."

"It's Hamilton House Beach. You've never been here, have you?" He was pretty sure she hadn't. This had been his thinking spot in high school. He'd have noticed if anyone else had trespassed on the Hamilton property and hung out back here.

Gemma ducked her head. Looked away.

"You mean..."

"It was the only slightly illegal thing I ever did. Besides, I asked Mary Hamilton for permission after the first couple of times, so technically, I wasn't trespassing after that."

"I just can't believe I never saw you down here."

"I was pretty good at hiding." She smiled. "I saw you, though."

Matt didn't know how to react to that. He'd cried down here more than once, cried that his mom had left them, that his dad has spiraled so far down that he hadn't known how to help himself, much less the son he'd been left to take care of.

She didn't say anything about any of it. But he knew when he met her eyes that she knew.

"I prayed for you. Back then."

There was nothing to say to that. He nodded, then walked away.

When he came back, he took a deep breath, turned his mind back to the case. "You wanted to know what's next."

"Yeah, I do. I've never been good at being on the defensive. Either I run away and forget this ever happened, or I want to do something about it. Be proactive."

He could see why she'd be good at marketing. Once she put her mind to something she was a go-getter. Someone who would do whatever it took to make sure the job got done.

"The first thing we should do is look back at that first case."

Exactly what neither one of them wanted to do. But there was no getting around it. It was still too soon to know for sure if Gemma was right about the body's identity, though Matt was hoping Shiloh and the forensic specialist from

Savannah would be successful in exhuming him today. If so, they could learn something on that front soon. And if Gemma was right, then the case was tied to her past. To *their* pasts.

"That sounds so simple, but how are we supposed to do that? You're just going to walk into the police department, walk out with that file, and no one is going to think that's odd? I want to keep it quiet that I know anything about that body. Maybe a few of the officers who were around back then will make the connection, and I can't do anything about that, but I don't want to spread this around. Not now, when I'm trying so hard to be someone besides the girl who saw a crime being committed."

"I can do it without people asking questions. Trust me, no one notices half of what I do."

"And once you get the file, we'll look at it together? You're going to share information with me?"

"I'm going to do what we need to do to solve this case."

She nodded. "And then?"

"And then we'll have to take that as it comes." A breeze rustled through the trees, unexpected on a day that had been mostly calm. Matt saw Gemma jump, noticed the tension clench back into her shoulders. "And, Gemma?" He hated being the one to say what he was going to say, but someone had to. "Please don't let your guard down. We're taking this a step at a time, because at any second our status quo could change. This guy is after you. He could take a shot at you, try to kill you somehow, in the next minute. Or tomorrow. Or when we're least expecting it."

Gemma said nothing, just nodded slowly and looked off into the expanse of ocean in front of them without saying a word.

Being at the beach with Matt had messed with her emotions more than she'd expected. Telling him she'd prayed for him… Those had been some of the most heartfelt prayers of her life. She'd really believed that God would step in, give Matt a happier family to grow up in.

Instead, his dad had gone to jail.

Sent there by the very girl who had prayed for better for Matt. Her faith hadn't known how to respond to that. It hadn't been long afterward that she'd left Treasure Point. At the same time, she'd also left the church.

Neither one of them said much on the walk back from the beach toward the house. What was there to say? Their history ran too deep for words, too deep to pretend like every step on that beach, through these woods, didn't bring up nightmares for both of them.

Matt finally broke the silence when they neared the construction site. His voice wasn't the quiet, contemplative tone he'd had on the beach. It was the in-charge-police-officer voice she'd noticed he used when he was working.

"Have you seen the old barn?"

"The one near the old house that they used as a garage?"

Matt shook his head. "This is an *old* barn, really just pieces of rotting wood now." He pointed out the spot. "You'd think as old as it is, it would have seen some interesting events. I don't know any stories about it, but you could ask Shiloh, or Mary Hamilton. Chances are that either of them would know."

"Shiloh?" Gemma didn't see why the crime scene investigator would know anything about the property. Especially since she was relatively new to town—she hadn't been there when Gemma graduated high school anyway.

"She was a history professor before she moved here, believe it or not. I know she's looked into some of the history around this area—some for a case she was involved in and some just for fun."

Gemma made a mental note to talk to Shiloh sometime…maybe. She'd be a useful resource, sure, but Gemma still wasn't sure how their meeting this morning had gone. And hadn't

Matt said the other night that Shiloh was one of the ones who doubted her story of being attacked the other night? The last thing she needed this time around with this case was to surround herself with people who doubted her.

"Thanks for letting me know."

"If we turned right here, we'd go deeper into the woods, where a network of trails—"

"I know. I've been on them."

The change in her tone must have caught his attention, because he turned to look at her, curiosity raising his eyebrows. "Is that where…?"

Gemma nodded.

"Oh. I never knew exactly."

Awkward silence settled around them for a few seconds. Then finally, Gemma took a deep breath and turned right. "Let's go, then."

"I thought you'd want to avoid it."

She met his eyes, only for a second, but long enough. "You deserve to see it if you want to. And maybe seeing it will help me remember that it's just a place. Nothing that has power over me anymore. Besides, it might jar loose some memories, help us with this case."

Without waiting for his response, Gemma started off down that trail, reminding herself that it was a piece of land. Nothing more. She felt her steps slowing a bit as she approached.

"You okay?" Matt's voice behind her startled

her at first—she'd begun to slip into memories—but once she recovered she appreciated the reminder that she wasn't alone.

"Getting there." Right now and as a whole. She was going to be okay with this part of her past—eventually.

Her phone buzzed in her pocket but she ignored it, turned to Matt. "Does seeing it change anything for you?"

"What do you mean?"

"I don't know." And she didn't. She'd just wanted to know how he felt. Maybe it was their pasts being so oddly linked, or being here alone in the woods, but she felt as though despite their obvious differences in background, they understood each other. Except right now she couldn't put herself in his position, couldn't picture how seeing this spot would make him feel, since this was where his father had been arrested.

Instead, all of Gemma's emotions swirled around her own memories. The fight she'd witnessed not far from here. The words yelled after her as she'd hurried through the woods to escape, making more noise than she'd wanted to. Shouted promises that if she told anyone what she'd witnessed, she'd end up dead.

She'd told the authorities anyway, had wanted to do the right thing—but no one had believed her. So she'd pushed the words from her mind for ten years, only struggling against them in the middle of a dark sleepless night here and there, when they liked to plague her. Now, of course, she could hear them again, the knowledge that there had been teeth behind the words making her all the more terrified. They hadn't been empty threats. The man who'd said them was willing to kill. Had *already* killed. Wouldn't hold back from killing again. She had a lingering headache today from last night's events that would remind her.

As though she needed reminding.

"What about you?" Matt walked toward her, feet crunching on the overgrowth.

"I feel..." She wasn't sure she had the words, but her heartbeat pounded harder, faster, at the idea of finding words to explain to Matt what she'd never been able to articulate to anyone, not even her family. "Sad. I feel like..." Like she'd lost part of her identity there, which was silly, really, since nothing so awful had happened to her on this spot. A man had lost his life and all she had suffered was a sprained ankle. But when she'd run, when she'd returned to town, she hadn't been the same Gemma Phillips that had left. No one would think of her from then on as a pretty girl, a good student, someone who loved literature more than math, who played the flute in the marching band.

From then on, she'd been Gemma, the Witness to a Crime.

And to much of the town, that was all she could ever be.

"Feel like what?" Matt asked, his voice betraying the depth of his curiosity for her to finish her sentence.

She shrugged, as if it didn't matter, even though they both knew it did. "I feel as if I left here a different person, or at least everyone assumed I was different."

"I don't know if I ever thought that." He met her eyes. "I never saw you any differently."

Something in the way he studied her made her breath catch. Did he really mean that? When he looked at her, did he see *her*, not just what she'd gone through?

Gemma wasn't ready to deal with that. She looked away from him, searching her mind for an excuse to busy herself doing…anything besides talking to him anymore. Because no matter how little sense it made, no matter how much Treasure Point was the last place she'd look for a man to start a relationship with—and Matt O'Dell the very last man she'd expect to be interested in—she was afraid if she stood here face-to-face with him for any longer, she'd spill all her secrets, show him her whole heart. Then want him to share his.

Then she remembered. Her phone had buzzed earlier. Relief relaxed her shoulders. She shoved her hand into her pocket. Text message.

I see you remember where you found us. Then you also remember that I warned you about what would happen if you told anyone what you saw. I haven't forgotten. And I keep my promises.

Gemma swallowed hard. Read the first line again: "...you remember where you found us."

He saw them here?

Now?

"He's watching," she whispered, grabbing Matt's arm. Her eyes searched around her. To the right, and then she circled around all the way, scanning the greens and browns of the trees and the forest. She couldn't see anything that looked unusual. But she'd grown up in the South; she knew how camouflage worked. With good camo and some cover, he could be mere yards away and they'd never see him...

Would he shoot her here, in broad daylight? Or would he try again to make attempted murder look like an accident—like he had last night in the office?

"Wait, Gemma, why?"

"I'll tell you later. Let's go."

This time she didn't wait for his response, just took off running down a trail through the woods, heaviness settling over her soul, chased by the knowledge that being here had changed her *again*.

And not for the better.

SEVEN

Gemma refused to say a single word until they'd been in his car for at least five minutes. The farther they got from the Hamilton Estate, the more she seemed to relax, but when Matt glanced at her now and then he could see that she was biting her lip as she watched the country pass by through the window. Her expression was a mix between a frown and something else—contemplation?

He'd give his last dollar to climb into her mind right now and know what she was thinking.

"Are you going to talk to me, Gemma?"

She started, as if she'd forgotten he was there, then shifted slowly in the seat to face him. "He sent me another message."

The rush of anger and frustration toward this mystery man was so strong that Matt could have hit the steering wheel, but after years of learning to control his temper lest he end up like his father, he took a breath and exhaled long and slowly instead. "When? Wait, when we were in the woods?"

She nodded.

That explained at least part of her behavior—the sudden running and the whispers about someone watching them.

It still didn't explain why she'd pulled away before she'd gotten the phone out. Her withdrawal had been as obvious to him as her literal running. Their conversation had scared her somehow. Because of something he'd said? Or because they were having it in the first place, the two of them?

"What did it say?" Matt tried to keep his voice level, hoped that him maintaining some sense of calm would help her be calmer. It was worth a try.

"He saw us. He said he saw us and reminded me that he's going to kill me." She shook her head, looked away again. "He promised me he would a decade ago, if I talked. And I did, I did it anyway. And now…"

"You're not going to die." He contradicted her conclusion before she had the chance to say anything Matt didn't want to hear. "And I think you're the bravest person I've ever met."

"Brave?"

"You've been called that before, surely. When you testified?"

She shook her head slowly. "No. I don't think anyone said that. No one seemed to appreciate it at all."

Which didn't make sense. She'd helped the town be a safer place. Because of her, stolen goods had been returned to the rightful owners and criminals had been locked away before they could cause any more harm in and near their town.

Oh. But she'd shattered the illusion for too many residents. She'd been a visible reminder that things like that *did* happen in Treasure Point. That they happened everywhere because the world wasn't perfect and people were greedy.

That. That was why people treated her differently.

"I'm sorry, Gemma."

She shrugged.

"Let me take you home for now. I'm going to call Clay, get him to hang out near your house to make sure you're safe while I finish out my shift."

"You're not done?"

"I'm working a little overtime tonight. I need to go into the police station to report the text message you just received and see if they discovered anything new about the body."

Gemma nodded. "Okay."

"Unless you want to come with me."

She shook her head. "The police department is the last place I want to be right now, but thanks. I'll be okay as long as you're sure Clay will be close by, watching."

"He will be. I'll be back home in an hour, two tops. Meet me back over there in two hours and let's talk about the case a little bit more. Hopefully I'll have more to share then."

Matt pulled into her driveway. "Let's go in. I'll check the house and then wait while Clay gets here." He punched the screen on his phone. Clay picked up quickly.

"It's Matt. Can you come to Claire and Gemma's house, maybe sit nearby in your car and keep an eye on things while I finish up at work?"

"Sure. I'll be right there."

No questions asked. *That* was a friend. Matt may not have too many of them, but the ones he had were genuine, the hard-to-find level of good.

Once Clay was there, Matt climbed back in his car and drove toward the Treasure Point Police Department. He still had the feeling that Gemma had more information about the case that could help him, but he wasn't sure exactly what it was.

"Anything new on the body?" he asked when he walked in. They'd managed to pry it from the Georgia clay late that afternoon and the ME had been ready to take it away.

Shiloh looked up from where she was making case notes at a table. She nodded in the direction of the chief's office. "Davies and the chief are talking to the ME now."

And as long as this was his case, Matt was going to be talking to him, too. He knocked on the chief's closed office door—something he couldn't remember doing before.

"Come in."

Like Shiloh had said, his two superiors were in there with Dr. Kevin Downs, the ME from Brunswick. Matt addressed his question to the chief. "Anything new on the body, sir?"

He nodded. "You should be here for this anyway. I thought Lieutenant Davies would have notified you." He glanced at the other officer.

Davies looked a bit chagrined. "I should have tracked him down, sir. I apologize."

"This is his case, Lieutenant. Don't let a slipup like this happen again."

"I won't, sir."

"As I was saying…" Dr. Downs cleared his throat. "The decomposition of the body indicates that it's been buried at least five years. The body itself was down to just bones, with a few scant scraps of fabric from clothes that hadn't finished decomposing. I'm going to take the remains to Brunswick, get started on finding out what I can. Today I wanted to know if there's anywhere you want to start looking to identify the body. As far as things like dental records go, it's quicker if you already have an idea of who the deceased might be."

Lieutenant Davies shook his head.

"Check the body against the records for Harris Walker," Matt spoke up.

"Walker?" The chief's eyes narrowed. "Drifter type, used to come to Treasure Point now and then years ago?"

"Yes."

The ME looked pleased to have a name to work with. "All right, I'll start there. Expect a call by morning, if not late tonight, Chief."

"Thank you, Dr. Downs."

Davies looked at Matt—stared him down, actually—as Dr. Downs left the room. "How did you know that?"

"I'd rather not explain it to you right now. Could I talk to you privately, Chief?"

The chief nodded. Just that quickly, Davies was gone, too—although not looking too happy about it—and the two of them were alone.

"The case ten years ago, the one where the group of men was arrested, tried and then imprisoned for stealing historical artifacts and antiques..." Matt described it in as much detail as he could without mentioning his dad. No need to draw attention to the fact that he was technically connected to that case, even though he hadn't been involved.

"One of the biggest Treasure Point has had."

"Yes. Well, I ended up talking to Gemma Phillips, who was a witness in that case, and she suspects she knows who the body is. That's the name she gave me."

"Do you know why she thinks the body might be Harris Walker's?"

Not enough to share yet—and certainly not without Gemma's permission. "I'm working on getting a clearer picture."

"All right. Well, it's all we've got for now so we may as well follow up on it." The chief's eyes narrowed. "I'm trying to remember who worked that case. I don't think they're here anymore. I think most of the men have either retired or moved on to bigger departments in places like Savannah, or I would connect you with them to talk through the case."

Let him talk to people who'd investigated that past case? So that meant...even if this current case, *his* case, was connected to his dad's, he was still going to be allowed to take the lead on the investigation? He was scared to ask. But the words came before he could stop them—he'd never been good at being sneaky or going behind people's backs.

"Sir, I'm still the lead on this case? Even if it does tie into that one?"

The chief nodded. "I don't see any reason you wouldn't be."

Sure, make him say it. "My…dad…sir…"

"Isn't you. And he's in jail. His part in this appears to be over and entirely in the past. The man we're after now is another matter entirely. If he's really threatening Gemma Phillips's life, he's not your father, since he's in prison, so I see no reason why this case would be too personal for you to be in charge of it."

"Thank you, sir. I won't let you down."

"I know. This is it, Matt. This is your chance. I know you can do it."

Matt was pretty sure he walked a little taller on his way out. He couldn't let the chief down.

Time to go talk to Gemma.

"You headed home?" Shiloh asked him from across the parking lot.

"Yeah," he answered. Most of the other officers who'd stopped by during the day to see the crime scene were gone now.

"Meeting Gemma?" Shiloh asked casually as

she packed crime scene equipment back into her car.

"I am."

"Be careful, Matt. I heard some things today... No one is saying this case is for sure linked to the one she testified in, but with the proximity of the body to that crime scene, it's gotten people talking. I just worry about how trustworthy she is."

"You're still pretty new here, Shiloh." Not like Matt. Matt had McIntosh County blood running through his veins. His family was Treasure Point from way back and he'd grown up breathing the salty, marshy air and splitting his time between the woods and the ocean, like any good Southern boy. "You don't know what happened then. And no one knows Gemma like I do."

There. He'd said it. The words that made no sense, even to him.

Just as he might've guessed, Shiloh's head snapped up at that declaration. "You're not just interested in her because of this case."

Matt shrugged. He'd said enough—too much—and wasn't going to keep going. But he knew it was true. There was something about Gemma that made him feel connected to her in a way he couldn't describe.

Shiloh shook her head, slammed her trunk

shut and brushed her hands as if she was getting rid of dirt. Or maybe just ending the conversation. "I hope you know what you're doing."

Driving home, with past memories mixing with mental pictures of the crime scene excavation today, wondering how he was going to sort through Gemma's perspective when he hadn't figured out what his own thoughts were on this case yet, he hoped he knew what he was doing, too.

Some of his doubts faded once he got home, changed and headed to his shed. He was in the middle of finishing up another ocean kayak, something he enjoyed not just for the finished product, but for the stress relief it gave him to work on the boats in progress, create something with his own hands.

Matt dived back into his current project, letting his mind work on the case as his hands worked on the kayak. He wasn't sure how long he'd been working when Gemma showed up. He only knew he'd forgotten to eat dinner, or go out to meet her.

"Hello?" Her voice echoed a little. Matt looked up to see her shadow in the doorway. "Sorry to barge in, but I knocked and you didn't answer. That's when I noticed the path over here."

She sounded so apologetic, as though she'd

interrupted something important. Not many people knew he did this in his spare time, but it wasn't a secret, either. It just…was.

"It's no problem, come in."

Her footsteps clicked on the concrete floor and Matt's smile grew a little when he realized she was wearing heels. City life must have rubbed off on her.

"Oh, wow. This is beautiful." Her eyes widened as she approached the kayak. She studied it for a minute, then looked up at him. "You built this?"

"I did."

"May I?" She reached for the kayak and at his nod, ran her hand over it.

"It's as smooth as it looks. You seriously built this?"

"I did." Matt shrugged. "It's no big deal." He shifted his weight a little, looked toward the door. He hadn't meant for them to talk about the case out here. First, because he didn't like people making a big deal out of things like this—if people were going to admire him, he wanted it to be because he'd done something worthwhile, like bring justice and keep people safe on the job, not because of a silly hobby. Second, this was where he relaxed. He'd rather keep the case separate. It was with that in mind that he spoke up again, before she could say anything else. "Mind if we talk inside?"

"Oh, sure." Gemma stepped away from the kayak, removing her hand. "I'm sorry, I didn't mean to make you uncomfortable with my going on like that…"

"It's fine. I'd just rather not be out here when we're discussing the case. It's…more of a laid-back place out here. Inside keeps things professional."

He'd added that last line mostly for himself, after noticing too many times how feminine and lovely she looked in heels. Her hair was down, loose curls hanging around her shoulders, and everything about her looked approachable, inviting, appealing.

Not a good combo in a person that close friends like Shiloh were warning him to be careful around. Of course, hadn't he stood up for Gemma several times already, insisted that he knew her true character?

And he did. Time to stop letting himself doubt that at all.

"After you." Matt grinned at her as he motioned for her to leave the shed first.

Gemma smiled back at him, full and brilliant, and he had to swallow hard and remind himself that they were working on a case together. Nothing more.

* * *

Gemma had felt like an intruder from the moment she'd stepped into that shop. And no wonder. He obviously poured a lot of time and care into those kayaks. It was almost like seeing a glimpse into some part of him inside that he kept hidden. She pushed down the feeling of hurt that he clearly hadn't wanted her to stay long in his private space. He was right—they should keep things professional.

"Want any coffee?" Matt asked as soon as they were inside the house. Gemma took the offering for the olive branch that it was.

"Sure."

Neither of them said much as the coffee brewed, so the dripping of the coffee and the occasional call of a bird outside were the only sounds in the silence. Gemma walked to the window, peeked through the blinds and looked out at the marsh and the river beyond.

"You've got an amazing view. I didn't notice last night. I don't think I'd ever close these windows."

"I don't usually."

That was all it took, that one comment from him, to remind Gemma that the windows were closed on her account. Because someone out there was watching her. Wanted her gone… whatever that took.

"We've got to find the guy after me," she muttered. "I'm not going to keep living this way." But for now she let the blinds close. No need to take risks that weren't necessary.

"We will." Matt said it like a promise.

"I hope you're right." She walked back to the couch and sat down, then took the coffee cup Matt offered her not long afterward.

"So. You thought talking again tonight would help?" Gemma couldn't think of a more smooth way to open the conversation.

"I wanted to tell you what I found in the case files. I haven't gotten to read all of them yet, but I do have a list of places that artifacts and antiques were stolen from. And I know what the stolen items were, in case that helps us any."

"Really?" Gemma had never known. They hadn't been discussed in detail in the part of the trial she'd been present for. Because of some legalities, she'd only been allowed to be present during the times she was testifying, and her parents had done a thorough job of sheltering her from newspaper articles about the case, so she didn't know all the details. "So what were they?"

"Maps."

"You're kidding."

"No, they were searching for and stealing old maps. Think about it and it's brilliant. Even if someone saw them with the stolen items, no one would see one and guess it was valuable—"

"How valuable are we talking?"

"Up to thirty thousand dollars."

Gemma almost spewed her coffee. "For one *map*?" She shook her head. "Yeah, I can see why they chose maps, then."

"So I want us to make our own map and plot out the places that had maps stolen from them. It would be helpful to learn more about the targets. You said that the argument you overheard was because Harris wanted more money—that was why he was threatening the other man. That makes me think that the killer must have been the man in charge—the one who found out about the maps, coordinated the team to steal them and decided how much each of them would be paid. If we find out who knew where to find the maps and how to steal them, we might find our killer. So to start with, let's map out the locations that were broken into."

Matt rifled through a desk in the corner of the room, walked back toward Gemma with pens and paper. "I know it's not much, but I figured at least we're doing something that may help."

She needed to feel like she was making progress as much as he probably did. "All right, let's do it." She reached for the case file.

Matt snatched it away. "I'll tell you the addresses, if you want to make the marks on the map."

"You don't want me reading those case files. Why?"

Gemma couldn't read the expression on his face right now. It was too odd a mix of too many emotions. Almost like he was fighting with himself. And maybe protecting her from something?

She didn't ask again. And he didn't say. They stayed focused on creating maps of the locations where things had been stolen, and after an hour or so, Gemma told him she had to head home.

"I've got a lot of work to do in the office tomorrow. I'll probably hole up there for most of the day if you think that's relatively safe."

Was it her, or did he look relieved that they didn't have plans to spend time together? "It shouldn't be a problem. Either me or another officer will be patrolling the whole time."

"Okay…good. I guess I'll go, then."

Matt didn't argue with her. Every time she'd seen him since they'd been reunited, it seemed like they'd taken two steps forward in their friendship. Tonight was the exception. The entire thing felt like two steps back.

EIGHT

Matt knew that the clouds gathering in the distance, coupled with the scent in the air, meant that a storm was coming. He liked storms when he could sit at home on his deck and listen to the rain, watch the lightning like it was his own private fireworks show—but tonight he was working a rare night shift. He didn't like working in bad weather.

Too often people didn't take the danger of the storm seriously and then ended up getting hurt by driving too fast on slick roads. Sometimes they even got stuck in floodwaters in the time or two a flash flood had swelled the banks of Hamilton Creek. And then he and other police and firefighters had to risk their lives to get them out of the trouble they'd caused.

A low rumble in the distance confirmed his thoughts about tonight.

This was a night he didn't need.

His shift started at 11:00 p.m.—an odd shift

for him—so he had a while before he had to be in. He'd already grabbed a quick nap.

Matt looked at his phone. Thought about the idea he had. But calling Gemma when he didn't have anything new to ask her or report about the case would look suspiciously like he just wanted to talk to her because he enjoyed her company.

But last night had left him confused, to say the least. He still wasn't sure how he felt about seeing her in his shop, looking over the kayaks he was working on. For some reason it felt like their relationship had gone one step further, like she knew him a little better, and he'd been extra reserved the rest of the night because of it.

Matt wasn't sure why. What was his deal? Fear of rejection? Fear that Shiloh and the others might be right, and Gemma couldn't be trusted after all? Fear of messing things up with the one girl in town who looked at him and *didn't* seem to see his father? Maybe all three. But if there was one thing he couldn't stand, it was feeling like he was making decisions based on fear. Besides, hiding from Gemma wouldn't help him solve this case. If he felt nervous about calling her, then that just told him that he should be spending more time with her to get this awkwardness out of the way. He picked up his phone.

Just a few punches of the buttons on the screen and her phone was ringing. "Gemma, it's Matt."

"Hey." The soft accent in her voice was untouched by her years in the city. She still sounded like home. "What is it? Did you find something this afternoon?"

He shook his head even though she couldn't see. "No." This whole plan was feeling stupider by the second. But there was no graceful way to back out now. "I was calling to see if…if you might want to go to dinner with me tonight?"

"Dinner?"

Her voice said this conversation felt as weird to her as it did to him. And yet…she wasn't saying no yet, was she? "That fish and barbecue place off the highway, A Pig and a Pond, is pretty good. Have you been there since you've been back?" He wanted to take back that last sentence as soon as he said it. He was pretty sure that was the last place high-class, cultured Gemma would have been since she'd been back in town.

"Claire and I went last week, actually. I'm a sucker for fried catfish." She laughed and Matt relaxed. Smiled a little. "I'd love to go with you tonight."

Really? "Great, I'll pick you up in about an hour if that works?"

"I'll meet you there if it's okay."

Because she had something to do before-hand? Or because she wanted to keep it more casual, make it feel less like a date? Either way, Matt was fine with it. "Sounds good. I'll see you then."

They met in the parking lot an hour later and walked inside together. A familiar country song played over the speakers when they walked inside, the twang of the steel guitar matching the atmosphere of the place perfectly. Matt cared more about the food at a place than the style, so it didn't bother him that the plain brown tables and forest-green chairs looked like they'd been pulled straight from an old-school cafeteria. "Does over here work for you?" He motioned to a table near the window, since this was a seat-yourself kind of place and he liked the view of the pond.

Gemma nodded. "Looks great."

They sat down and a waitress came with menus. Matt started reading the choices, even though he was pretty sure he'd get a barbecue-fish combination plate, like he usually did.

Across the table, Gemma hadn't moved.

"Everything okay?" he asked her, just in case, expecting her to laugh at his overprotectiveness. How it had sprung up so fast was anyone's guess, but it had. He hated the idea of her being hurt or even uncomfortable.

She didn't respond. He focused all his attention on her now, looked her over, but couldn't see anything that could indicate a problem.

"What's wrong?"

Gemma wouldn't meet his eyes. Wouldn't move her gaze at all, actually, from where it was fixed on the menu in front of her.

Finally, a whisper.

"I feel like someone is watching me."

The words robbed him of his appetite and slowed everything in the room down, made him hyper alert. Matt swallowed hard, stayed in his seat, did his best not to react to her words in a way that anyone would notice. If she was right, then this situation had the potential to go from bad to worse if he wasn't careful.

"Can you tell who? Or even which corner of the room?" For that matter, was it someone inside the restaurant at all?

Gemma shook her head. She looked up at him and he saw the panic in her eyes, the way she'd turned pale. Whether or not she was being watched, she was reacting badly to the idea of it, sinking deep into what looked to him from the outside like a full-on panic attack.

"Nothing is going to happen right now, not while I'm sitting here with you in this restaurant. I've got my duty weapon, and besides, I see two other officers in here. Right now, we are going to see if we can narrow it down at all, maybe come closer to figuring out who is after you, but nothing bad is going to happen."

It was a lot to promise, Matt knew even as he said the words, and he prayed that he'd be able to keep his promise. He thought the tension in Gemma's shoulders eased slightly at his words. But he knew it wasn't enough. Threat aside, their dinner was over for now. He needed to get her outside in the fresh air, get her thinking about something besides her panic, or things were going to get worse.

Matt motioned to the waitress, ignoring Gemma's eyes, which widened when he made any movements at all. It was almost as if she was afraid to move and draw attention to them, lest the man or woman watching her know she was there, which was of course illogical reasoning…but who could reason with fear? Nobody could. It took God working to overcome it at a person's core.

"Could I get two sweet teas to go? That's going to be all for us tonight." Matt kept his tone casual, smiled naturally, and the waitress didn't ask questions. When she returned with two large disposable cups—a hallmark of a country restaurant around here—he left enough money on the table to cover the drinks and a tip, and touched Gemma's arm. "Come on. We're leaving."

This was the tricky part. Matt had scanned the room, hoping he'd be able to figure out who'd caused the panic reaction on Gemma's part, but he couldn't be sure. The killer whose voice she heard was a man—but he might have a female accomplice. His voice had sounded familiar to her, so he was probably someone who lived in the area ten years ago, but that didn't necessarily rule out the out-of-towners. In short, there was no way to know who might have been watching her…or if anyone was at all. Still, he wasn't going to discount her feelings—there had to be a reason for them—so he did his best to stay between her and most of the people they had to pass on their way out of the door. And he ruled out a walk by the pond to calm her down. He still didn't know if someone could have been watching from outside.

But he had to do something.

Matt helped Gemma climb into his truck—which had seemed a better choice for a dinner like this than the patrol car he often drove even when off duty. She still wasn't talking and she still looked like she might be sick.

All he knew to do was drive her to where he went when life didn't make sense.

So he took her to the Hamilton Estate, led her

down the path in the woods to his beach…*their* beach, apparently. Matt didn't know why he'd never noticed Gemma down there back in the day. He guessed maybe because he'd wanted to be alone and so he'd assumed that he was.

He sat down in front of a large piece of driftwood. It served as a sort of backrest for them to use as they sat in the sand in front of it.

Several minutes passed. Matt would watch Gemma for a few seconds, then realize that might be contributing to her stress, and he would look away, before feeling like he needed to check on her and glance that direction again.

He guessed about five minutes of sitting on the beach passed before she looked at him with a hint of a smile. When she did, he let out the breath he'd been holding.

"I think I'm okay." The words were soft, a little wavery, but she nodded her head with certainty like she'd decided to be okay and therefore would be. "I'm sorry."

Matt shook his head. "No need to apologize."

"It happens, you know. Since that day in the woods…"

"Often?"

Gemma shook her head, smiled a little more. "Thankfully, no. They're very rare. Although since being back in Treasure Point I worry they're getting worse."

* * *

She didn't know how long they'd sat there, but she knew that the sun had set with a brilliant peach-and-pink flourish and darkness had settled before either of them looked at the time.

She finally pulled out her phone. "Ten o'clock. Didn't you say you had to work tonight?" Gemma thought Matt had mentioned something earlier about working a night shift.

"Ten? I've got to get going. I'm on at eleven, and the guys getting off their shift get cranky if the night shift is late. They're ready to go home and sleep."

He probably was, too, Gemma thought—not to mention hungry, since she'd kept him from getting dinner—but he'd never say so. Different as they were, that part of him reminded her of her dad.

"I probably won't see you tomorrow," Gemma said as they started down the path through the woods. She shivered a little in the dark, wishing now that they hadn't stayed out so late. "I'm guessing you'll sleep most of the day, and then tomorrow night I've got dinner at my parents' house. They asked if Claire and I could both come—somehow we haven't managed to get together for a meal since I've been back in town, so..."

"I hope dinner goes well."

She laughed. "My family is pretty easygoing most of the time, unless they're concerned for one of us." Her voice trailed off as she said the last part. "I wonder what the chances are that my parents haven't heard about everything going on?"

"Slim."

"Scratch that, then. Dinner will be very, very long."

They didn't talk much more, just made their way back to Matt's car and climbed in. Matt started driving toward town.

"I left my car back at the restaurant," Gemma realized. "Could you drop me off at it before you head to work?" The idea of driving home alone in the dark bothered her a tiny bit, of course, after the debilitating fears of earlier. But she needed it to get to work in the morning.

"No problem. I'll check it out for you. Not that I think anything is wrong, but just in case."

Gemma nodded, thankful he'd thought of that. Thankful he cared enough to think it.

The trip down the highway and then back to the restaurant went quickly. Her unease about getting in the car dissipated a little—she'd forgotten how close she'd parked to a streetlight. At least the situation had that going for it.

"Thanks for tonight," she said to Matt, smiling a little. It had been even more like a date than she'd anticipated. Did that mean a good-night kiss? Her heart thudded a little at the thought, but she didn't make any moves toward him—she was a good Southern woman after all—and he just smiled at her, making no attempts, either.

"Thanks for coming. Be safe tomorrow, okay? I don't like the idea of you being without police protection for the whole day, but Clay's got to work and I've got to catch at least a quick nap or I won't do the case any good."

"I should be fine. I'll just be in the office, and someone will be patrolling there, even if it's not you, right?"

"Right," Matt said with a nod. "It should be okay. Just don't let your guard down too much, okay?" He seemed to realize what he'd said. "But don't panic, either."

Gemma laughed. "I'll do my best."

"Mind if I have your keys to look at the car? Wait here and I'll check it out." Matt climbed out, inspected the car, even started it for her, and then motioned for her to join him.

"Looks good to me. I'll follow you home."

Gemma slid her phone out of her pocket and checked the time again. "Quarter till eleven and you're not in uniform? I think we'd better split when we get into town. I feel safe enough knowing there are people around and it'll take me, what, two minutes from where you turn off the main road to get myself to Claire's?"

She could tell Matt was considering it, but he didn't look particularly happy about it. "You're right. I don't have much of a choice at this point, just please, be careful."

Gemma nodded. "I will be."

Matt stepped away from her door, but stayed nearby. Gemma climbed in and only then did he get back into his truck. She smiled and drove out of the parking lot, thankful to have him and his headlights in her rearview mirror, following her back toward town.

The darkness of this stretch of highway had just started to make her uneasy when the lights of Treasure Point came into view. She let out the breath she'd been holding, waved toward the back window when Matt turned off to head home to change and eased the car toward Claire's house. Almost there. She'd just curved around the bend when she noticed a car on the side of the road.

SUV. Dark. No lights on.

Just as she passed it, its headlights flared to life, and the roar of the engine revving was loud enough even for Gemma to hear through closed windows. The anxiety she thought she'd beaten earlier came back in full force, but she fought it this time, refused to let it control her.

The vehicle sped closer, closing the gap between them. Gemma wanted to deny that the person driving was intending to cause her harm, wanted with all her heart to pretend it was a coincidence. But she couldn't. Not with the SUV almost touching—

The thud of metal and the shudder that went through Gemma's car and her body confirmed her worst fears.

The killer hadn't stopped trying to end her life.

Gemma jerked her wheel hard left, then right, just to see if she could unsettle the car behind her at all. The SUV didn't waver in its pursuit and hit her again, this time threatening to make her lose control over the car. Gemma took a deep breath, let it back out. If she could just hang on for another thirty seconds, she'd be over the narrow bridge for this last crossing of Hamilton Creek. That was the only thought in her mind—she couldn't go into the creek.

She held on tight, then released a breath when she made it over the bridge. Three—maybe four—football field lengths separated her from town. She could do this—

One more crunch of metal, this one harder, jerkier. The impact threw her forward and to the right, and the wheels spun with her. In one long, slow motion moment, she felt as though she'd been pulled into a kaleidoscope of darkness and headlights and breaking glass as her car flipped and flipped and rolled off the road into the grass.

Then everything stopped.

Gemma wanted to cry, scream—something, *anything*—but no sound would come from her throat.

Matt. She needed to call Matt. He shouldn't be far. She lifted her right arm, which took more effort than it should have—and patted around in the passenger seat where she usually put her purse. She had to move slowly, carefully, because one of the windows, it was too dark to see which, had broken and pieces of glass lay everywhere. Where was her phone? The impact and rolling had knocked everything around...

There. It was on the floor, which was the ceiling since she was suspended upside down.

She took a deep breath, punched in Matt's number.

His voice was serious from the start. As though he realized there was no reason for her to call when she'd just seen him unless...

"I've been in a wreck, Matt. He hit my car and it flipped...just after the second Hamilton Creek crossing on the way to Claire's house. I think he sped past me when it happened, but

I just don't know and I'm alone and I can't get out." The last part frustrated her more than she could say. She should be able to do *something* besides hang there worthlessly while she waited for someone else to save her.

"I'm on my way."

And so she waited.

The sound of humming bugs that had welcomed her back to Treasure Point the other night on her sister's porch, the ones that had seemed soothing and peaceful, now seemed like notes out of tune, a cacophony that only grated on Gemma's nerves, made her clench her teeth tighter.

There was no welcome to be found here. Not as long as someone lurking in the shadows wanted her dead.

NINE

"Gemma!" Matt's voice shouting, along with the sound of his footsteps running toward her, finally broke the monotony of the cicadas and frogs.

He'd come.

"Are you okay?" First his words again, then his face at the window, his eyes taking her in, assessing her for injuries. Gemma knew she had a few cuts and bruises, but was fairly certain it was nothing serious.

"I'm okay. I think." Her voice was steadier than she would have expected it to be. "I just want to get out and go home."

Although she wasn't sure where home was. Really what she wanted was to start over, to go somewhere where the past wouldn't hunt her down and try to make sure she died. But that wasn't an option. She had no resources to fall back on—nowhere else to go. All she could do was find who was behind the attacks, make sure justice was served both for herself and for the man she knew had already lost his life to her tormenter.

Several other cars pulled up, but Matt stayed close by, his presence helping keep her calm. *God, are You watching? Why are You letting this happen?* Gemma wasn't sure if she'd meant to pray, but the questions rose to heaven anyway. Once, she would have waited for an answer. Tonight she kept her eyes closed, but didn't try to continue the prayer beyond that.

She wasn't sure how long it took to free her, but she was eventually pulled from the wreckage of the car.

"We're going to need you to answer a few questions," the police chief said. The fact that he'd come himself underscored the seriousness of the situation. Gemma nodded. When he started asking the typical questions about what she'd seen, what had occurred, she answered everything as best she could.

"Do you believe now that I'm not making these things up? I know some of the officers thought the other attempts on my life were coincidence at best, or maybe things I'd set up. But you see the paint." She gestured to the scrape of dark paint down the side of the car.

The chief nodded. "I see it." He looked over toward Matt. "I know Officer O'Dell has believed you the whole time. Looks like I put the right man on this case."

"Thank you, sir."

"Do what you need to do to keep her safe, okay? Shiloh will process this and have the car towed, Gemma. O'Dell, take her to her sister's house for now, then you come back."

"Yes, sir."

Neither one of them talked much on the way home. There was almost too much to say, at least in Gemma's opinion, so she stayed quiet.

Claire was asleep when Gemma arrived, not waiting up since she'd thought Gemma was out on a date and not fighting for her life again. She'd have some explaining to do in the morning when the car wasn't in the driveway, though...

Gemma tried to sleep, knowing she needed to, but tossed and turned for most of the night, and when the clock finally showed that it was almost five, she decided she'd tried for long enough to sleep and got up. She'd be paying for the lack of sleep later, for sure, but what could she do?

"There you are. I was starting to doubt you were really living here." Claire looked up from what she was mixing—Gemma could only hope it was her cinnamon rolls—and shook her head. "You've been crazy busy. Work? Or avoiding me?"

Claire's eyes narrowed as Gemma moved farther into the kitchen lights. "What happened to your arm?"

Ah, yes, the cut on her left forearm.

"I need you to remember to stay calm." Gemma started as she moved to the coffeemaker, which had just beeped, and poured each of them a cup of coffee. She handed Claire hers first. "And probably to sit down. Don't overreact."

"What am I not overreacting to?" The tension in her voice had built to that "older sister" tone she used so well. And too frequently.

"I was in a wreck last night. Someone hit me on purpose, tried to kill me." Gemma was surprised at how easy it was getting to deliver that news. She was still just as terrified, but this was becoming normal. She hated that, wanted more than ever to solve this case and make it all stop. "The car flipped—they had to basically cut me out of it. Repairs aren't going to be easy, or cheap. I may need to borrow your car at some point, if you don't mind. I'm sorry."

"I don't care about you borrowing the car, Gemma, of course you can. I care about you! This is all tied to that case from when you were in high school?"

She nodded.

"And someone who has already murdered at least one person is trying to kill you?"

Another nod.

"We've got to talk to Mom and Dad, get them to hire some kind of private security detail."

Gemma laughed. "Claire, the last thing I'm doing is involving Mom and Dad in this, and the second to last thing is hiring any kind of security. For one thing, they wouldn't be people I knew or trusted, so I can't see that working out well at all."

"And the police here are people you trust? After they didn't believe you back then when you *told* them someone might have been killed?"

"Those people aren't working here anymore. And even if I'm not sure about some of the officers who are there, the chief seems good. I like him. And I know I can trust Matt."

"Matt O'Dell." Claire's voice was flat, then built back up with emotion. "You're serious. I know you said he was working on the case, but you're happy about that? You *trust* him? Have you forgotten that's the case that finally sent his dad to prison?"

The bite in her sister's tone surprised her. Gemma had forgotten, somehow, in the past few days of getting to know him again, that her family had viewed Matt the way the rest of the town viewed Gemma—as someone whose whole identity was wrapped up in events surrounding that trial. Gemma had been judged as questionable because of her vague association with the criminals, even if she had testified against them. Matt carried more than that. He carried all of the sins of his dad in the eyes of the community. Though obviously some had accepted him since he had to be respected to a degree to be a police officer, she imagined there were those who still saw him as the boy from the wrong side of town—well, if Treasure Point had one of those—who would probably turn out to be just like his no-good father.

She'd forgotten that her family would probably feel that way—not because they were the type to judge others, but because they were protective of Gemma. They knew how badly the trial had hurt her, and were biased against anyone associated with it. And Gemma was bringing him to dinner at their house tonight.

Before dropping her off in the wee hours of the morning after she'd given her statement to the chief, Matt had told her that he wanted to go with her to her parents' dinner, provide extra security, especially on the drive to and from their house, which sat a bit on the outskirts of town. Gemma hadn't had the bravery to fight him in the aftermath of the wreck.

Maybe she could cancel the dinner altogether. But no, knowing her parents, especially when they heard about the wreck, they'd just bring dinner to her. There was no getting around this. Only getting through it.

"I haven't forgotten. But he's different than you think," she insisted. There were so many things Gemma could have said to show what Matt was really like, but those were the only words that would come to her. Instead, her mind kept seeing pictures. Matt last night, staying near the window of the car and giving her a comforting, encouraging face to look at as Gemma was slowly set free. Matt smiling at her, teasing her. Matt by her side at the Hamilton House Beach…

Gemma swallowed hard, tried to change the expression she knew must be on her face as she realized that her sister's scrutiny was going to reveal the truth that she'd been trying to hide, even from herself.

"You are not falling for him." Claire paused for less than half a beat. "You are. You are falling for *Matt O'Dell*. Could you have picked anyone more wrong for you?" Claire stood up, taking her coffee with her, and started to pace the kitchen.

"I don't know what I am—" Gemma opted for full honesty, but Claire cut her off before she could continue.

"No. Just no." There went that tone again. Did older sisters always think they knew best, even when both of you were adults and capable of making your own decisions?

"He's different than he was in high school, Claire. I'm different. Maybe it's not such an awful idea."

"It would take a lot to convince me of that."

More mental pictures. Gemma smiled. "Maybe he'll convince you." She couldn't believe the words even as she said them, especially considering Claire's obvious disapproval. Gemma had always tried to make decisions her family was proud of—it felt like she tried harder than most people did to win their approval. Maybe it was common when someone had been adopted. She couldn't draw from others' experiences, only hers.

Something in her heart wavered. Surely they'd see Matt had changed, right?

"We'll see if that's even possible." Claire shook her head again, looking so smug that Gemma didn't care too much about making her happy at the moment; she just wanted that look off her face.

"He's coming tonight."

Claire's eyebrows raised. "To Mom and Dad's?"

Gemma swallowed hard.

Clare just shook her head. "This is going to be fun."

The rest of the day passed slowly as Gemma counted down the hours until what would probably be one of the most awkward evenings of her life. Had she warned Matt sufficiently that her parents were incredibly picky about who was "good enough" for their daughters, even just to have as friends? And that their attitude toward him was likely to be less than friendly?

Finally it was almost six and Matt's car pulled into the driveway. Claire had planned to ride her bike from her coffee shop, so only Gemma had needed a lift. It would take insurance a week or two to work out what was to be done with Claire's car. Gemma was fairly certain it was totaled, but she couldn't know for sure.

"How was today?" Matt looked like he'd aged a year or two overnight. He clearly hadn't gotten enough sleep, and there was a new seriousness in his eyes.

Worry for her had put that there. Gemma wasn't sure how to feel about that.

"It was fine. You're sure you're ready for my parents' house?"

"I'm sure." He laughed. "How bad could this be?"

* * *

Bad. The unspoken answer to the question he'd asked earlier was *very, very bad*. The white plantation-style house that towered above them, situated at the edge of the marsh on a large spread of land, was fancier than any place Matt had ever visited as a guest, except *maybe* the Hamilton House before it had blown up. And that place had at least had some warmth to it, real history that had worn down some of the furnishings until they were no longer shiny and new. This house just looked like money.

He could think of a dozen places he'd feel more comfortable than right here. He glanced to his right, where Gemma stood looking up at the house with a similar level of trepidation. "You grew up here?" he asked. He'd known they were worlds apart in high school, but somehow even in a town as small as Treasure Point, he'd never known exactly where she lived—just known it was a nice place near the marsh.

Gemma nodded.

Matt let out a low whistle. *Nice* was an understatement. This place was—

"Hello, dear." A well-dressed woman in her early fifties opened the door, looking like she'd just stepped out of some Southern women's magazine—Matt hadn't had a mom long enough to know any by name—and looked at Gemma with pure love in her eyes. Matt made a note of that, out of habit from his job, he guessed. You never knew when assessing someone's motives based on their apparent character could come in handy.

Then she turned to him. "Did someone whistle?"

Gemma coughed. Matt felt his face go red.

"Sorry, ma'am." He stuck out a hand. "Matt O'Dell. Thank you for letting me come with Gemma tonight to make sure she—"

Mrs. Phillips's eyes hadn't left his face, so he knew she didn't see what happened. Which was good, because she missed Gemma stomping her heel down into the tips of his toes. He winced, swallowed hard and stopped speaking even though he was in the middle of a sentence. She didn't want her parents to know he was just here for her protection? He shifted his eyes her direction, but she was looking away. Pretty intentionally, it seemed like.

"Well, come in anyway. And no need to introduce yourself, Matt. We know who you are."

If only those last words seemed encouraging rather than a little derisive.

Mrs. Phillips turned and entered the house, seeming to expect them to follow.

Matt looked at Gemma then. Before he could

ask her why she'd stomped his toes blue, she shook her head, her expression mortified. "She's never been like that. I mean, they've always had money, but they've never been…"

"Above people?" He forced the words out, then forced himself to shrug his shoulders, hoping if he did it enough times in his life in response to treatment like that, then it wouldn't matter anymore.

Too soon, they were inside the house, Matt fighting the urge to turn and leave with every step he took forward. If he weren't so concerned about Gemma, he'd be out of there in less than a heartbeat.

But he'd been right to insist on coming. This place was a logistical nightmare for someone trying to stay out of a stalker's reach, like Gemma was. First, the place sprawled and he'd noticed several outbuildings on the way in. Buildings like that quickly became a liability in a scenario like this, since they provided a place for criminals to conceal themselves before an attack, or somewhere for them to hide a person—or worse, a body—if they'd abducted someone. Then there was the staff. Had he known people still *had* cooks? So far, that was the only other person he'd seen besides the family, but that didn't mean there weren't more people around who were employed by the Phillipses. People with easy access to attack Gemma with outright violence, or more subtly by slipping her a drug to knock her out or even poison her. And he couldn't exactly ask how many staff there were without seeming more low class than they already viewed him.

For the sake of the confusing feelings he had when Gemma was around—he wasn't ready to figure out what those were yet—he'd kind of hoped they'd forgotten his family's reputation. That maybe they would be willing to accept him for the man he was.

So much for that.

"So, Matt. You're a police officer?"

"He is, one of the best Treasure Point has, in my opinion."

Mr. Phillips looked at Gemma with amused eyes. "Let the man answer for himself, sweetie."

"Yes, sir," he answered, feeling like he was still expected to. "I've been an officer for the past eight years."

"You enjoy the work?" This question was from Claire, who smiled a little as she asked it—maybe at least Gemma's sister was willing to give him a chance.

"It's rewarding knowing I'm doing my part to keep Treasure Point the town we've always loved."

Mr. Phillips nodded.

"And, Matt," Mrs. Phillips said, "do you find it's difficult for you to do your job, considering?"

He felt the muscles in his legs tense, wished he could walk out of the room and be done with this. Instead, he flexed his fingers at his sides, comforted himself with the fact that he could work on his latest kayak when he got home.

"Considering what?" He kept his words slow and measured as he met her eyes.

She attempted to play off the awkwardness of the question with a little laugh and a dismissive wave. "Oh, you know. Your history."

"I don't have much interesting history, Mrs. Phillips. I went to the same school both of your daughters did and I believe it trained me pretty well for this job. That's really all the history that matters, isn't it?"

She let it go after that.

But the questions didn't ease off, and most of them were no less insulting. Gemma's face grew paler by the minute, but she didn't say anything. Neither did Claire.

His phone ringing in the middle of what would have been an incredible peach cobbler if his stomach hadn't been churning actually turned out to be a relief. He slid it from the phone holster on his belt loop and glanced at the screen.

Treasure Point PD.

"Excuse me, please."

He opted to head for the front door so he could step out onto the front porch to take the call, rather than go to an empty room. He was half-afraid if he did the latter Mrs. Phillips would accuse him of stealing some little trinket. He'd been surprised by her coldness, if only because it didn't fit the genteel-hostess role that would have matched the house. He'd have expected more politeness, at least the pretend syrupy stuff, from her.

He shut the front door behind himself and answered the call. "This is Officer O'Dell."

"Hey, Matt, it's Clay. We got a call from a guy at the Brunswick Police Department. He's working the scene of a robbery right now and says it's something you'll want to see. He didn't have your phone number, so I told him I'd pass on the message."

His and Gemma's ticket out of here.

Matt let out his breath. "Great. Thanks for letting me know."

"Anytime." Matt knew that Clay meant it, too. He was a good guy, easy to work with and someone Matt trusted.

The Phillipses looked at him quizzically

when he began explaining that he and Gemma needed to go, seeming shocked that he would leave before dessert was over, even more shocked, it seemed to him, that he'd speak for Gemma, too.

"Thank you for dinner," he finished as he glanced Gemma's way. She set her napkin on the table, scooted her chair back and stood, as well.

"Gemma, you can stay. Can't you?" her mom pleaded. "Your dad can drive you and Claire both home later. She shouldn't ride her bike at night anyway."

Gemma shook her head. "No, I'm leaving with Matt. I'll be back by…" She glanced over at him. "As soon as I can." At least she understood he wasn't likely to let her far out of his sight after that car wreck.

Her dad nodded. "We'd like to see you soon."

"I'll do my best." Matt heard the promise in Gemma's words.

He followed her to the front door, said goodbye and thanked them one more time—though he wasn't sure why since their hospitality had been anything but genuine—and finally they were outside. They walked to the car, where Matt held Gemma's door open for her and explained what the call had been about.

"That estate sale I mentioned I wanted to keep an eye out for? The one in St. Simons?"

"Yeah?"

"They were setting up for the sale and noticed that sometime between yesterday morning and tonight, all of their maps were stolen. They have limited security there, but it sounds like they might have enough to get us a lead, if we work for it. A crime scene team from Brunswick is there now. I've got a buddy on it who knew it might tie to my case and called into the station. He asked Clay to pass the word along to me if I wanted to have a look."

"Then, let's go."

Matt raised his eyebrows. Well, what harm was there in letting her come? As long as she stayed in the car so she was out of the way of the investigative work, he knew his friend wouldn't mind. "All right, let's go."

They drove back into Treasure Point to get the highway, and then took it south toward Brunswick and St. Simons. The sun had set sometime in the middle of their dinner—apparently wealthy people liked to eat late—and the sky was fully dark now. Matt glanced over at Gemma, glad she was with him, and tried not to think about the last late-night drive she'd taken. About how differently things could have turned out.

When they reached St. Simons, he pulled into a gated community—frustrating that their private security hadn't managed to keep criminals from stealing objects of value—and followed the directions he had to a large house at the end of a cul-de-sac.

He parked the car, eased his door open. Gemma followed suit. Matt shook his head. "No."

"No?" She raised her eyebrows, challenge all over her face. "What do you mean?"

Yeah, judging by how her parents doted on her, there was a good chance that wasn't a word she'd heard much growing up.

"You can't come out into the middle of a crime scene, Gemma. You're not an officer. In fact, if anything, you're part of this investigation and one of the very people who *shouldn't* be here."

Her dark eyes seemed to smolder a bit at that comment. Then, just as fast, the anger was gone and she was nodding. "You're right. I'll stay."

Matt didn't argue. Just nodded, told her he was glad she understood and walked away.

No way Gemma planned to stay in that car. But what *did* she plan to do?

He found his friend from the Brunswick PD, Derek Dallas, near the three-car garage.

"Thanks for calling, man." Matt stuck out

his hand. "I heard you thought this might be something I needed to see."

Derek shook his hand. "Yeah, I think it is. The things stolen were a little odd. There were a lot of items of value that were going to be sold this weekend, everything ranging from rare books to fine china, even some paintings by some Southern artists whose names any art critic would recognize. But none of that was taken. We aren't sure if the perp ran out of time or if there's something else going on here."

"And the only things missing?" Matt asked, even though he was fairly sure he knew the answer.

Derek was already nodding. "Maps. Could be coincidence. They were probably the least secure items. The guy liquidating the estate is a distant relative of the deceased—he didn't even realize the maps were all that valuable. He said that he thought some of them might go for a few hundred dollars."

Matt winced. He knew from researching the old case that many old maps went for thousands. Easily. Some for enough thousands to buy a car. "Does the seller know which maps were stolen? I mean, did they keep an inventory list or anything so we know what the maps were of?" Just in case they were wrong about maps themselves being the treasure this criminal was drawn to. It would also be useful if they could find out just how rare or valuable the missing maps really were.

"I don't believe so, but we can ask. He's inside, practically beside himself that he let this happen."

They headed toward the double front doors of the estate, Matt shaking his head that he was headed into a house full of opulence for the *second* time this night. Here he'd thought normal people lived in houses just a bit better than the run-down trailer he and his dad had called home. Turned out half the people in their corner of Georgia had something like what he would call mansions.

He followed Derek across the grand foyer into a living room, hoping he wasn't getting mud on the deep Persian rug that stretched across the hardwood floor. That room connected to a dining room, where they skirted around a large table. Derek pushed open a small swinging door. The kitchen?

In the kitchen was a seating area with a small round table and four chairs. Two of them were occupied already. One with an older man— probably in his early seventies—and one with a young woman who looked almost like...

Matt raised his eyebrows. "Hello, Gemma."

The man, whose back was toward the door,

swung around. "Oh, hello, Officer. This young woman was just asking if she could get me anything. I was about to say I'd love a mug of coffee, but first I was telling her about what happened. She hadn't heard the details, you know."

Matt wondered why the man hadn't thought it odd for a stranger to enter the house and offer things. Too trusting? Possibly suffering from some degree of dementia?

Or could he be the man they were after himself?

Suddenly it wasn't a crazy thought. Seeing her in here, alone with the guy—who looked to be in pretty good shape for his age—frustrated the tar out of him. Hadn't he told her to stay in the car? How hard were those instructions?

No. Surely he was getting paranoid at this point.

Still, the possibility tugged at him. Nagged him.

"I asked you to stay in the car."

"You know this young lady?" the man at the table asked. Derek looked fairly curious, too, something Matt couldn't blame him for.

Matt nodded. Didn't offer any other information and Derek, thankfully, didn't ask.

"I'll get his coffee, if no one minds," Gemma offered. "I actually was trying to help." She said the second part more softly, as if she thought Matt wouldn't believe her. And she was partially right. It was hard to imagine she hadn't had any intentions of investigating after the way she'd treated his request in the car. Then again, he didn't exactly blame her for it. Wouldn't he have done the same thing in her position?

"Might as well." Derek shrugged. Then he turned to Matt. "Did you want to ask him about the list?"

"Sir, I'm sorry to hear about your maps. I wondered if you might have a list of the ones that were stolen?"

"A list?"

"Often historic maps have titles or descriptions that correspond to what's on them, how old they are."

The man shook his head. "I'm sorry. I don't know any of that. Just that there were some old maps."

Matt looked at Derek, shook his head slightly. Derek seemed to catch his meaning, because he stood and Matt followed. "I think that's all I wanted to ask." Matt tried to mask the disappointment in his voice. What had he been expecting—that the man would have a detailed description of the thief and know where to find him? No, he hadn't been dumb enough to expect something like that. But he had hoped that investigating here tonight would bring them one step closer to figuring out who had stolen them, since it was very likely that whoever had stolen maps from this estate was the same man who had been part of the gang Gemma had helped break up and send to prison.

"Sorry. I'd hoped you'd find out more."

"It's okay. It was worth checking out. Get in touch with me if you find prints besides this guy's, okay? I want to know everybody who's touching something here. Landscapers, household staff, everybody."

"Gotcha. It's no problem."

Matt shook the other man's hand. "Thanks again for calling."

Gemma must have seen him preparing to leave, because she met him over by the truck.

"Ready to go?"

"Yeah." She was quiet for a second. "Sorry. I just couldn't..."

"I know."

And they climbed into the truck without another word. Matt glanced over at Gemma when they were off the neighborhood roads and back on the highway. She was sleeping—trusting him to keep her safe while she did so.

They had to find the guy who was after her soon. Because he seemed to know where

Gemma was at almost every moment, which meant that even if he was doing his best, Matt still lacked confidence that he could keep her from her stalker for much longer.

TEN

Gemma reread what she'd just written on the notepad in front of her, thinking through her ideas again for marketing the Treasure Point History Museum. Within the town, it would market itself for the first few weeks at least. Everyone would want to see what was there, know what all the fuss had been about during the construction process. The trouble with the townspeople would be making this a place they'd want to come see more than once, which was necessary because to survive it would need a year-round operating plan.

South Georgia, Treasure Point especially, did have some winter visitors, especially people on their way to Florida, so they couldn't afford to close and miss potential customers. But on the other hand, there wasn't as steady a stream of tourists then, so they'd be depending on the people of Treasure Point to visit the museum regularly.

What would draw them?

Gemma tapped her pencil against the paper and frowned. Then signed and started jotting down ideas.

1. Their history. They need to take ownership.
2. Changing exhibits?
3. Interactive corners—get them involved.
4. Kids programs?
5. Special events/programming—holiday-centric?

They weren't bad ideas. She needed to think about them more, though, let them grow in her mind a little. She'd found in the time she'd been working at the big corporation in Atlanta that she was good at meeting deadlines, at working under pressure, but her best ideas came when she didn't force them, just let her mind work on the problem and then waited to see what it came up with.

She needed a walk. Gemma slid her shoes back on—she'd taken them off when she was sitting at the desk—and headed outside. She waved to the construction workers, most of whom she recognized even after only a short time of working nearby. There were a few unfamiliar faces, though. Gemma started into the woods, wishing Matt was there to keep her company. Instead, another officer had taken his place patrolling the museum earlier today and Matt had sent her a text earlier that he was following up on some possible leads tied to the estate sale in St. Simons.

Gemma's cell phone rang and she stopped just short of the woods trail she'd been about to take. Unknown number. She hesitated, finger hovering over the screen, poised to answer. Then she shook her head, slid it back into her pocket. She was tired of letting herself be terrorized. Either this was a telemarketer, or it was a wrong number, or the killer wanted to threaten her again and she wasn't in the mood to let him today. Matt had already tried tracing the phone from the text messages, but it was a disposable, pay-as-you-go phone bought with cash. For all intents and purposes, it was untraceable.

She abandoned the idea of walking into the woods alone. It probably hadn't been a good idea in the first place, but the mysterious call, timed so perfectly, had convinced her that it wasn't smart. Instead, she turned around, walked back to the construction site. A stack of materials had been moved just in the past few minutes, forcing her to walk a bit closer to the work site than she normally did, since she usually tried to stay out of their way.

She looked up at what they were doing. They seemed to be working on the framing, and it looked like there were guys everywhere—on the ground working on various things and walking on beams across the structure to work up there. Gemma shook her head as she looked down. She didn't mind heights, but she didn't think she could treat working on top of a building quite as carelessly as these guys seemed to.

Gemma heard her phone ring in her pocket. Again? She looked down and started to pull it out of her pocket.

Movement caught the corner of her eye. She turned enough to see something light coming at her, but it was moving too fast for her to get completely out of the way. Instead, she lifted her arm over her head, did her best to dodge.

Impact. In her wrist, sending electric shocks of pain down her forearm. She heard a scream—more high-pitched than hers should have been—only to realize it *was* her scream.

And the pain. She'd never felt anything like this, but she tried to keep her mind off it even as she hit the ground and instinctively rolled away from…whatever had hit her.

"Help!" she yelled.

Ryan Townsend, the construction foreman,

was the first one to reach her, though she'd seen people running all over the place. "Are you okay?"

"My arm. Someone dropped something..."

He helped her up. "I don't see anyone working nearby. But it must have been an accident."

Gemma was already shaking her head. "No, I don't think so. You don't see anyone suspicious at all?" She gritted her teeth against the pain in her arm while she waited for him to answer.

"I don't see anyone around here but my guys. Sorry, he must have gotten away."

Gemma nodded. Of course he had. He was one step ahead of them, all the time.

It took all the good manners within Matt to knock on the door of Gemma's house when all he wanted to do was throw it open and make sure she was really okay.

Claire opened the door, looking like he felt. "Is she okay?"

"She's fine. The doctor says that her wrist is broken, but all things considered..." Claire trailed off. Matt knew what she meant. A broken wrist was one of the best things it could have been when they considered all of the possible outcomes from the "accident."

"Where is she?"

"On the back porch. I tried to get her inside…" Claire shook her head. "This whole thing is changing her. At least I don't remember her being this stubborn when we were kids."

Matt started off in the direction Claire had indicated.

"Oh, and, Matt?"

He turned around.

"I'm sorry for how my parents treated you the other night. I'm not sure I'm your biggest fan myself, but…well…it wasn't fair of them. Or kind."

"Thanks, but not your fault. We can't be responsible for our parents' actions."

Understanding passed across Claire's face. She nodded. "Maybe you're right. I'll keep thinking about it." She left the room and Matt walked toward the back porch.

"Should you be out here surrounded by windows?"

"He's not going to shoot me. I think he's still holding out hope that the police department doesn't believe that someone's really after me, even after the evidence from the car wreck, so that he can pass off my death as an accident. Shooting would be too obvious. He's being very creative—this last attempt with one of the beams from the construction site…I can see how people might have assumed that was an accident. No wonder not everyone believes me."

"Your sister told me she thinks this is making you more stubborn, this whole…situation." He could think of a whole list of other things to call it, but *situation* seemed the least inflammatory at the moment. Especially since he was accusing her of being hardheaded, something people didn't usually take well.

Gemma's head shake was vehement. "Not true. I've always been like this, just…kept it hidden."

"Why?"

She shrugged. "Why do we do the things we do? I don't think we realize half the reasons."

She was right. Matt nodded, studied her for a minute. "You know what I think?" he began.

"What?"

"I think your whole life you've been trying so hard to make sure you don't disappoint anybody that you kept half of Gemma locked away in case she could possibly offend someone."

She looked like she wanted to contradict him. But she didn't. Instead, she was moving toward him, first lifting her face just a bit toward his, then leaning in his direction.

Matt didn't know why it took his mind so long to realize what she was doing. Maybe because it was so unexpected, now or ever. Gemma Phillips, starting a kiss with him?

But she was. And they were. And for the seconds that it lasted, he couldn't think straight. Or at all.

He was the one to pull away. He knew it was the right thing to do, even though it was something he'd probably beat himself up for later.

Gemma blinked up at him, confusion in her eyes, and for a split second he wondered if everything between them was ruined.

"I'm sorry, Matt."

"You don't have to be sorry—"

She cut him off. "I got a little carried away. You just seem to know me so well. Better than my family sometimes. About my parents the other night—"

"I know they mean well for you, Gemma. They love you with all their hearts, that's obvious to anyone."

"I...I know." She didn't seem sure to him. "But the way they talked to you..."

"They're your parents. Don't try to understand them or explain them or apologize for them, okay? Just know that they do what they do because they love you. I didn't enjoy meeting them—but I know their hearts were in the right place. They just want what's best for you."

It went unspoken that he was considered far from the "best."

And in a way, they were right. Oh, he didn't believe that his father or his background made him in any way unworthy to date Gemma, but it really wouldn't be best for her—or him—to get distracted with romance right now when they needed to focus on finding the man who was trying to kill her.

With that in mind, he took another step back, and saw in Gemma's expression that she understood he was deliberately putting distance between them.

"But…" Her voice trailed off.

"Let's not worry about it right now." Maybe he shouldn't suggest it.

Gemma took a minute to think, biting her lip for a minute, and then finally nodded. "You're right. We'll just…wait and see."

Matt nodded.

"Ahem." Intentional throat clearing from the doorway made both Matt and Gemma turn.

Claire's eyebrows were raised and the expression on her face—a cross between curiosity and concern—made Matt wonder just how much of their conversation she'd overheard and seen.

"Gemma, I just wanted to know if you thought you could eat. I made Brunswick stew."

"I'd love some."

Claire nodded and then walked away, leaving the two of them alone. But they sat in silence anyway, nothing more to say. Just Gemma sitting there looking wistful and Matt wishing there was something he could do to push all her sadness and anxiety away.

Unfortunately, wishing didn't do much good. Solving the case would.

"I've got to go," he finally told Gemma. "I'll see you…"

Gemma winced. "I'm supposed to take a couple of days off, according to the doctor. I don't know why, since it's just a broken wrist…"

Matt guessed it had something to do with the pain she'd be feeling as shock wore off. "So maybe not much for the next couple of days. I want to see you…" He felt like she needed to know that. "But I need to focus. Need to take advantage of the attack today to see if I can generate any more leads. I want to find this guy."

"Not as much as I want you to. Or me to. Anyone, really. I just want him in prison."

"I'm going to do my best." It had never mattered so much. This wasn't just proving himself anymore. This was Gemma's life. The pressure was on.

The first day he didn't see Gemma seemed to last forever. By the second day, he missed her but was neck deep in the case. And possibly making progress for the first time.

Evidence in the estate theft indicated that more than one person had been involved in stealing the maps. The news was unexpected—Matt along with everyone else had been assuming that one man was responsible. The idea that there were more people working with him...

Too many possibilities opened up at that point. Was the man they were seeking—the one directly responsible for the threat to Gemma's life—the one in charge? Or was he just a random part of a crime ring of some sort?

Or did more than one person want Gemma dead? The only reason to believe there was a single suspect was based on the assumption that it was the man Gemma had overheard arguing with Harris Walker, who'd ended up dead and buried on Hamilton land. That was another development these past few days—in addition to having his identity confirmed by autopsy, the Treasure Point Police Department had managed to dig up a few other things on the deceased. From the way it looked to Matt, Walker had been involved in the crime Gemma had seen, then argued with someone and ended up dead. Unfortunately, that was all he had.

Would Matt's dad know more?

He hated the question, wished his dad didn't factor into this at all, but he had to wonder. And would going to the prison where he was being held, even if it was for an official law enforcement interview, damage Matt's career? Mar the reputation he was trying so hard to build—the one entirely separate from his father?

His phone rang. *Chief* flashed on his screen. "Hello?"

"O'Dell. I need to talk to you. How soon can you get to the station?"

"I can be there in five minutes."

"I'll see you then."

Matt drove to the police station and walked into the chief's office. He hadn't been called in there many times. Matt tended to keep a low profile on the job—he didn't get in trouble for anything because he did his job well, took pride in it. But he didn't get called in to talk to the chief much, either, because he'd never worked any big cases like this or done anything noteworthy enough to be singled out for it.

"Good to see you, O'Dell." The chief stood from where he'd been sitting behind his desk. He shook Matt's hand firmly and motioned to the chairs across the desk. "Sit. I need to up-date you on the investigation into the wreck Gemma Phillips had the other day."

"What did they discover?"

The chief shook his head. "Shiloh can tell you the details about the paint markings, the damage and the rate of speed and what it proves—but what matters is that we're cer-tain someone intentionally caused that wreck. Which means that everything that's happened to Gemma which was initially…overlooked… should be reconsidered as probable attempts on her life."

What was he supposed to say to that? Hadn't they assumed so the other night? Matt didn't know, so he nodded. "Yes, sir."

"You were sure already, weren't you? No confirmation necessary." The older man's eyes narrowed slightly, but not in a negative way, just in a way that looked like he was consider-ing what Matt wasn't saying. He leaned back in his chair. Nodded his head like he'd decided something. "Tell me what you think, O'Dell. From the beginning."

"I think someone is after her, sir. From the first night after she got her new job, when someone locked her in the office and gassed her… That wasn't an accident. And nothing after it was, either. I think…no, I'm sure that whoever wants her dead would also like for us, the police, to believe that she is overreacting at the best. Deliberately deceiving us or being paranoid at the worst."

"We're past that now for sure. Since the body discovered does belong to the man Gemma claimed was involved in the smuggling ring, she's a confirmed witness in this case now. A homicide investigation. That's big. Full-time-security kind of big."

"What if… Sir, right now, her stalker thinks no one but me believes her."

"Okay. Where are you going with this, O'Dell?"

"If we put an officer at her house, her workplace, anywhere and everywhere, then someone watching her is going to notice security stepping up, going to know that we are listening to her, which would have us getting closer to finding him. For Gemma's safety, I think we should actually keep the security as low profile as possible here." As long as the chief was asking for his opinion, he was going to give it to him.

"Say we do that…I'm assuming you're going to provide security for her personally during the day. But what about nonworking hours? You have to sleep sometime."

Matt had already thought of this, too. "Shiloh

doesn't live far from her. I imagine she'd be willing to provide some backup if necessary. But I admit I don't have a good solution for nights."

"You're right about the necessity of a low profile, though. We let the killer know we're closing in, he'll know we're giving weight to her testimony and he'll pull out all the stops to silence her."

Matt couldn't think about that statement too long. The implications, the events that could take place…

The kiss made it easier to admit. He cared about her more than he should care about someone he was trying to protect as part of his job.

Although had keeping her safe ever really been about his job? Or had it mostly been about wanting to see her smile, wanting to know she was taken care of?

Matt focused back on work. On why he was here in the chief's office.

Another few seconds of silence passed and the chief finally stood. "Well, I don't know what else to say about this right now. Except that I think you're on the right track." He clapped a hand on Matt's back. "Keep at it. And don't let any of the other officers like Davies try to hone in on this. This is your case. Use their help as you need it, but you've done a better job at it so far than anyone else would have or could have. I'm glad we have you, Officer O'Dell."

And with that Matt knew for sure. He couldn't fail at this assignment. Not if someone was finally putting their confidence in him to do this job.

ELEVEN

Gemma had broken her wrist on Monday. By Thursday she was a little worried she was going to go crazy cooped up in the house.

"Anything I can get you?" Claire stuck her head into Gemma's room. Again. For the fifth time in the past hour. Gemma knew because she'd gotten bored enough to start keeping track, just out of curiosity. She'd also gotten into the habit of waving to Phil Winters, the mailman, every day when he dropped the mail off at their house.

Pretty soon she was going to get really desperate and take up a hobby. Knitting. Scrapbooking. Crossword puzzles. *Underwater basket weaving*. Anything to occupy her mind. Gemma laughed at herself, causing Claire to look over at her with her eyebrows raised. "You're sure you're okay?"

"I'm fine. Really." She was thankful that

Claire cared...but for the past two days she'd turned her coffee shop over to a college student who worked there part-time so she could stay home with Gemma, mostly to make sure no one broke in while she was napping and killed her.

It sounded absurd, but that was what they were worried about, wasn't it? No need to sugarcoat it for herself.

Her phone rang from its spot on the bedside table. It was a new phone—a cheap one from the Walmart in Brunswick with a pay-by-the-month plan—so only people she considered essential had this number.

Matt.

She smiled as she picked it up to answer. "Hello?"

"Sick of being cooped up yet?"

"Maybe," she teased, trying for a coy tone.

"Well, if you want to stay home..."

Gemma laughed. "Please get me out of this house. And tell me you've made progress in the case without me." Not that she didn't want to be needed. But it would be horrible to worry that the case had been stalled because of the past few days she'd spent napping away the pain from her wrist.

"I have. Little things, but they're piling up."

He hesitated. "I don't think it will be long before we find this guy."

"Why don't you sound more excited about
that?"

"Because the end is the hard part, Gemma.
In a case like this, all the puzzle piecing in the
world, no matter how hard it seems, isn't the
main event."

She heard the warning in his voice. The end
was the dangerous part.

Even more dangerous than almost dying of
carbon monoxide poisoning. Having her car
run off the road. The broken wrist, crushed
by the heavy lumber that could easily have hit
her head.

Gemma didn't want to believe that it could
get worse. She did, though. "Okay, I believe
you. Now come get me. I'm tired of sitting
around wasting time when I could be helping."

"I'm already in your driveway."

Gemma glanced down at her pajamas. "Give
me two minutes."

Three minutes later—hey, she'd been close
to on time—Gemma was out the front door,
wearing jean shorts and a sleeveless button-
down shirt she'd borrowed from Claire's closet.
Hopefully the cute shirt and the bracelet she'd
thrown on at the last minute made up for the
fact that she'd pulled her dark hair into a messy

ponytail, barely taking the time to run the brush through it.

Something danced in her stomach as she walked toward Matt's waiting car. She hadn't seen him since the kiss that neither one of them had been sure about. Did he regret it more now? Would everything be weird between them?

But no, here he was, eyes taking her in and face widening into a smile.

"You look good."

"Thanks. You, too."

And he did. The same uniform that only a few months earlier had made her cringe a little from her past experience with police officers only served to make Matt look more handsome. He was everything the uniform was supposed to represent—strength and confidence, but trustworthiness, too. And he was surprisingly thoughtful, as well. She'd always assumed he was one of those guys who took life as it came to an unhealthy degree. But he did consider his actions before he took them. She'd learned a lot about him in this past week or so.

Mostly that she'd been so wrong about herself and Matt O'Dell having nothing in common in high school. And that reuniting with him was one of the best things that had happened in her life so far.

"Get in. You're the navigator."

She did and they took off down the road. Gemma shuffled through the stack of papers in the manila folder that Matt had set in her lap. "What's all this?"

"Everything we've talked about so far with this case. Pull out the maps on top."

Gemma did as he asked.

"That's where we're going today."

"We're visiting all of them?" There were at least ten places they'd marked on the maps—locations that had reported stolen antique maps in the past fifteen years. Even though the initial case Gemma had testified in had only taken place ten years ago, they'd widened their search range a bit to make sure they didn't miss anything that could have slipped through the initial investigation.

"That's the plan."

"And what are we going to find?"

Matt shrugged, grinned with that smile she'd once found infuriatingly easygoing. "I guess we'll find out."

Gemma smiled, leaned back against the car seat and just enjoyed the ride. Moments like this, where the world felt almost normal, had been few and far between since she'd come back to town. And although she wasn't ignoring the threat on her life, she wasn't going to look behind her, hold her breath for every moment of the next few hours. No, she was going to do what she could do to be active in the investigation, help Matt, and be brave.

It was about time.

She'd no longer had the thought than the sun outside the window darkened, hidden all at once behind a cloud.

She wasn't going to let the weather dampen her enthusiasm, either.

The trip down the highway went smoothly, and even when they weren't talking, Gemma felt like she was soaking in the feeling of just being with him. Of not needing to say anything.

But when they turned off the highway onto a back road somewhere between Treasure Point and Darien, the country road wound through tall pine trees. The sun seemed even dimmer here, and somehow it dimmed Matt's mood, too. She looked over to see him frowning.

"What's wrong?"

Matt shook his head at first. Wouldn't answer. So Gemma tried again. "Really, what is it?"

"I'm just wondering what I was thinking now, bringing you with me here to investigate. Assuming I'm right that the guy we're after has robbed all these places before, that means that he's familiar with all these locations."

"So? Why would he come out here today?"

Matt's expression was still dark. "He's been following you pretty closely."

"But he only attacks me when I'm alone," Gemma argued.

Matt shrugged. "I don't have a good reason for worrying." He glanced over at her. "I'm probably just overreacting."

Gemma thought he probably was. She did have to admit, though, that once they slowed down in front of the first driveway, there was something eerie about seeing in person the places the thieves had visited with crime.

Even though she'd seen the evidence, watched them burying their loot, this made it more real.

Especially now that she knew for sure that someone had died because of this. Because of greed? Or had Harris threatened to go to the police after Gemma had started to run away, maybe having had second thoughts about being involved in the crimes?

It was possible Gemma would never know.

"Here's what we're going to do. I'll drive by all of the places on the map, like this, and we'll make a note of anything that stands out to us."

"Just characteristics of the houses, or should I be looking for something else?"

"You know, for this one I'd say it's very isolated, trees around the house, no close neighbors. All of those could be factors in why it was chosen. Think about it—there are antique maps all over downtown Savannah, but as far as I know, none of those houses were hit." Matt looked over at the map Gemma was holding. "No, all of the targeted houses are in smaller towns. So there's got to be a reason for that."

"Lack of confidence in small-town police forces? I mean, no offense at all, but couldn't it be something like that?"

"It could be. But I think there's more."

They drove to several more places. They all matched the characteristics of the first house.

Not one was in town. There were all perfect places to commit a crime without witnesses. Whoever was really behind those thefts had planned everything out, had thought carefully about targets.

The attacks against Gemma had also been carefully planned. Another indication that the same criminal was likely behind it all.

The recently robbed estate in St. Simons was in a gated community, something that didn't fit with any of the older targets, but even it was set back from the road, providing a bit of isolation.

"How did he find some of these?" Gemma asked after the second wrong turn they'd made trying to find one of the houses. "We were both born and raised in the area, and we're still getting lost. You'd have to be really familiar with this area not to get confused by some of the dirt roads, the roads with similar names…"

"I agree. But it doesn't narrow down our suspect pool much at the moment. There are plenty of people around here who could be comfortable driving around the boonies."

True. Gemma wished he wasn't right, but he was.

There had to be a way to get down to the question of *who* was after her.

"Last place," Matt said when they were leaving another isolated house. The clouds were out in full force now—the typical afternoon thunderstorm having gathered early today. Gemma was already bracing herself for the storm that was coming soon.

He pulled up to a parking lot near the river. Parked. Opened his door.

Gemma smelled the marsh's distinctive scent of salt and mud. She turned to him, eyebrows raised. "What are you doing?"

"Taking us to the last house." He nodded to an island across the marsh with a house that looked to her to be entirely abandoned.

"What's that? Is there something there?"

"*That* is the only house where witnesses interrupted the robbery itself." He shot a glance in her direction, looked away. "You…you don't know about this house?"

Unease crept like chills, leaving a trail of bumps along her arms. Gemma shivered in the Georgia July air.

"What about it?" She took a breath, waited for his answer. Thunder rumbled in the distance as the sky grew even darker.

Matt wasn't answering. Gemma waited.

Matt pulled his door shut again after the thunder, ready for the rain to fall. He'd planned for them to make the trip over to Whitetail Island in kayaks, which he'd brought over and hidden along the shoreline earlier this morning. They still probably could—most summer storms around Treasure Point were over as quickly as they started. They'd wait for it to pass and then go.

Would Gemma recover from what he was going to tell her as quickly as the sky was likely to clear after this rain? Matt wrestled with himself, with the words, with the weight of knowing she'd been ignorant about some things that had happened in the original case.

"Matt." Gemma's voice, insistent, steady, brought him back. She wanted answers.

He needed to give them to her. Except if he

did, she'd understand even more why his concern for her safety kept growing.

"You weren't the only witness to the crime ring's criminal dealings."

"You said that already. What happened to the other witnesses?" She hesitated for a second, met his eyes, her expression urgent. "I need to know."

Did she? Every second that passed was a second he regretted having said anything. But it was too late now. Besides, when he really thought about it clearly, Matt knew she needed to know. Had to be told just how dangerous the man after her really was.

He'd already killed two, maybe three times. No way would he hesitate to do it again.

If knowing that saved Gemma's life, he owed it to her to tell her.

Matt looked at her, sitting in his passenger seat and took a breath. "The couple living in this house was supposed to be at a party in St. Simons the night the robbery took place. Unfortunately they stayed home, no one is sure why, and they interrupted the crime. There were... signs of a struggle. Blood. The bodies were never found."

"But it's assumed they were killed?"

Gemma asked the question like she already knew the answer, kept her voice flat, almost emotionless. Matt knew her well enough to know that it meant she was feeling much more than she let on.

"That was the assumption."

She looked away from him.

"No, don't do that, Gemma."

"Don't do what?" She didn't face him when she asked the question.

Matt reached out, touched her hand, which rested on the armrest. When she didn't move it, he laid his hand on top of hers, wove their fingers together. "Don't pull away."

And she didn't. She turned back to him and he watched her eyes move from their hands, up his arm, shoulders, to his face. "It's what I do."

"I know it is. But don't."

She closed her hand, squeezed his fingers, then relaxed again. Exhaled. "So we're going to this house?"

She'd shifted the subject. But she hadn't moved away from him, hadn't even looked away. Instead of pulling away, she was attempting to move through the hard things they'd discussed. And she was doing so admirably. Matt was pretty sure Gemma was the strongest, bravest woman he'd ever met.

Rain started falling now, hard from the heavy clouds, pounding on the roof of the car, streaming down the windows.

"That was quick."

"Yeah. It was." Quick, but he'd known it was coming; it had been only a matter of time.

They waited out the rain in silence, hands still joined. Matt didn't know what that meant now or what it might mean later…didn't really need to know. All he knew was that he didn't want her to let go. And he sure wasn't going to.

"So…how are we getting to this island?"

"You know, I'm not sure about this after all, Gemma." She'd been through enough, hadn't she? Now he was going to make her go to another place charged with the kinds of stories that were the stuff of nightmares? The investigation wasn't worth this, not yet. It wasn't as if Matt had solid evidence that going there would help. This was only a hunch of his that might lead to nothing.

"No, I want to go. I think we should check it out. Ten years ago, the whole case was worked so quickly in an effort to make sure justice was served. We should make sure there's nothing left there to find."

Matt nodded. At least she saw his point. No one had heard from the people who'd owned the house—and though they were presumed murdered, no one knew for sure, and Matt had heard that the house had just been left to time and natural forces. Either they'd had no heirs, or the heirs hadn't taken care of the house.

"How are we getting there?" she asked again and he realized he hadn't answered her the first time.

"I thought we'd kayak. I brought some here for us earlier. Sound okay?" He hadn't actually confirmed whether or not she could kayak and she hadn't said the other night, when she'd seen the one he was building in his workshop.

Thankfully she nodded. "Yeah, I can kayak."

"We'd better go, then." Matt glanced down at their hands, not quite sure he was ready to separate them yet. But it would take a little while to get to the island, then there was the hike to the house to consider, then the time to explore. He hadn't packed food, just a couple bottles of water, so they didn't have unlimited time.

Gemma smiled at him, squeezed his hand with hers one more time, then pulled away. "All right. Which way to the kayaks?"

"Follow me."

They outfitted themselves in life jackets, then climbed into the kayaks. "Guessing you didn't make these?" Gemma grinned, obviously teasing since they were bright orange-and-yellow plastic.

"Good guess."

They pushed off and started out down the

tidal creek. The marsh grass surrounding them was tall, made it hard to see. Whitetail Island was still visible, even as low as they were with their boats in the water, but without a map—which he had brought—or good knowledge of the area, someone would never be able to figure out how to work their way through a maze of marsh grass.

"Left or right?" Gemma asked more than once when they came to places where the creek split. Matt would answer and they'd continue on, making their way to the island.

"Well, we know from visiting this house that it was definitely not a crime of opportunity," Gemma commented at one point. "The thieves had to really want those maps to come all the way out here."

"I agree. I think if we go back and look at evidence records for what was stolen from where we'll find that the maps from here had a pretty high value."

"I'd guess that you're right." Gemma exhaled with the effort of paddling. Then inhaled deeply. "Wow, that smells like home, you know?" She shook her head. "You don't smell that in Atlanta."

"What, the smell of decaying grass and mud?" he teased her. The truth was he loved the smell of the marsh, too.

From the playful smile she threw his way, he was pretty sure she knew that already. Of course she did—Gemma seemed able to understand things about him that he didn't yet understand himself.

"Right up here in this sandy spot." He pointed with his paddle and the two of them ran their kayaks up to the shallow water by the shore, then hopped out and dragged them the rest of the way. "I'll tie these up back here." He motioned to some bushes. "I don't think anyone but us is out here, but just in case."

"Right."

Her face had paled a little at the mention of other people possibly lurking nearby. Matt didn't like it, but couldn't do anything about it yet. He stored the kayaks just a bit off the beach, tied to some old bushes at the edge of where the sand turned to grass, then went back to Gemma. "Hey." He ran a hand down her shoulder, over the outside edge of her upper arm. "It's okay. I wouldn't bring you here if I thought we were unsafe in any way."

She looked unconvinced.

"Do you want to just go back to Treasure Point? I don't think there's any danger here, but I understand that the whole place feels..."

"Creepy."

That was an understatement. The entire island had a feeling of unease, of melancholy. Even the soft beach grass growing at the end of the shore seemed to make mourning noises instead of the normal swish that could sound so relaxing. It was a place that had seen too much sadness, and it felt to Matt almost like the land itself couldn't bear it.

It only made him more determined to investigate, to see if there was anything here that could help their case. Whether it had ever been proved or not, Matt was sure the couple who had lived here had been murdered. And they deserved justice. It wasn't just a fight for Gemma to be able to live fully—it was a fight to make sure these people hadn't died in vain, hadn't died quietly while their killer had gone free.

So much was riding on him doing a good job. So much more than his pride, although there was still that, too. He had to investigate this island; he could feel it deep in his gut. "I need to be here, to look around. But I promise you, Gemma, say the word and I will take you back and come on my own another day."

And he meant it, too. As much as what they were doing was worth sacrifices, it wasn't worth hurting Gemma, not even emotionally.

She met his eyes, seemed to see how much she meant to him—which scared the life out of him, but he'd deal with that later, shoved it aside for now—and nodded. "Okay, let's stay. Show me how to get to the house."

He reached out his hand. She took it.

And onto a narrow dirt trail through the tall grass they went.

TWELVE

Foliage had overgrown the back porch of the house. A place that Gemma could imagine having once been the scene of rocking chairs, of sweet tea on the porch in the evening, now looked spooky and decrepit.

The whole house itself felt like a warning. Everything inside her wanted to leave.

But hadn't she done that once already? Run from trouble and tried to start over? And here she was, a decade later, still not free from this.

Gemma was ready to be free. Whatever the cost.

"Matt?"

"Back here," he called from the direction of a falling-down outbuilding. Gemma thought she could see a path through the brambles. She glanced down at her cute running shoes, which she'd only worn outside of the gym a handful of times. They were going on a real adventure today.

"Coming!"

It was too fast for her to know what happened first. She was falling, backward, but hands were pulling her, she hadn't just lost her footing. She opened her mouth as a hand was clamped over it and felt the roughness of work gloves against her lips.

Gemma tried to fight, but her left arm was nearly useless because of her broken wrist. She reached her right arm behind her, to hit whoever was holding her, but the blows didn't seem to faze him.

She heard a low laugh. The same one she'd heard outside the door the night of the carbon monoxide poisoning. He'd wanted her dead then and he wanted her dead now.

Except this time he might get what he wanted.

She kicked as he dragged her, not going easily. Her heart sunk when he managed to drag her around the house and up the steps to the front porch. Matt was still around the back of the house and had no way of knowing which way she'd gone. How long before he wondered what was keeping her?

Gemma bit back a sob, tried to keep fighting even as her hands were bound behind her, the pressure against her broken wrist making it hard to breathe, much less move, without pain shooting through her.

When the blindfold went on, she knew her fight was over.

He dragged her again and this time she didn't fight him. She couldn't see where she was going—couldn't risk pulling away from him only to fall off the side of the porch or down stairs and badly injure herself. He finally let her go only to shove her to the floor. Gemma wasn't sure how high up in the house they'd gone, had lost count of the stairs they'd climbed.

She heard the low laugh again, then a door slamming. The door to wherever she was? And was he in or out of the room?

She had to assume out. She couldn't handle the thought of being trapped with a killer. Staying positive was her only hope of getting out of there.

Her heart pounded. As the pain in her wrist eased to a dull throb, she tried to think again, tried to figure out an escape. Gemma wasn't a quitter.

And then she smelled the smoke. Heard the crackle as the fire advanced.

Gemma threw herself backward against the wall, hoping beyond hope that the ropes binding her would catch on something, that she'd be able to get loose. She tried again, this time hitting her wrist so hard she had to pause for a minute. The smell of the smoke intensified, pushing her to think faster before it was too late.

Her blindfold. She had to forget her hands, do without them for now, and somehow get her blindfold off so she could at least look for a way out. She rubbed her face against her shoulder, loosening it a little, but not enough to move it away from her eyes. She turned her head, tried one more time on the other shoulder.

And felt fabric move. She pushed again, still hoping to get it off and over her head, but after another few seconds without progress, Gemma tried the other way. Even getting it down around her neck would make it possible for her to see.

There. She had it.

But the ability to see at this moment only overwhelmed her. The blindfold was gone, but the room was so full of smoke that she couldn't see clearly. She could make out a window, but the glass was shattered in some places, boarded up in others. Not a good escape possibility, especially since she didn't know how high up she was at the moment.

"Matt! Help!" she yelled, realizing that since

the man had let her go she could once again shout. But could Matt hear her over the fire?

Gemma lowered herself to the ground, walked on her knees to keep the worst of the smoke—which hovered higher—from overwhelming her. If she had her hands, she could crawl, but that wasn't an option right now. She had to work with what she had.

The door seemed far away, even though it was only a few feet. She moved toward it as quickly as she could, trying to decide as she did so whether she'd take the risk and open once she reached it.

Gemma glanced back at the window. Saw flames. Was the fire coming from multiple directions, or was her stalker still out there, setting more fires as he waited for them to overwhelm her?

"Matt!"

She kicked the door open after only a few tries, thankful to her gym in Atlanta for all those fancy exercise machines that people in Treasure Point would have made fun of. Smoke filled the hallway, too, and Gemma was disoriented, unsure where to find the staircase. She ran right, which took her into another room, this one filled with…

Maps? Maps covering the walls. Not antique ones. *Current* ones, with locations on them.

She took one second to stare, tried to absorb all she could in case she did get out of here and this room was destroyed. But surely it couldn't be relevant, could it? This was an abandoned house. Just a piece of the past.

But that was an X where Claire's house was.

And X where she'd been run off the road.

An X at the Hamilton Estate.

More X's she didn't have time to look at because the smoke was making her dizzy, burning her eyes, reminding her that none of this would matter if she didn't get out alive.

Gemma turned left, moved as fast as she dared with almost no visibility, and tripped down several stairs. Stairs! She was headed the right way. She moved more deliberately, down, down, down.

And ran into...

Matt.

"You're okay!" His voice was panicked. Relieved. Loud and yelling in her ear and the best thing she'd ever heard. "We have to get out of here!"

She knew. The house had looked near to crumbling before the structure had been damaged by the flames. "Where's the front door?" she yelled back at him, the roar from the fire seeming to suck the volume from everything in the room except the flames themselves.

"Down more stairs. This is the second floor."

Had she been pulled that far?

"My hands are tied. I can't go very fast."

Matt reached behind her, made an attempt at the knot and shook his head. "Too tight. We'll have to wait until we're out to untie you." He coughed, pushed his hand between her arm and her waist to guide her. "Come on."

They rushed down the last set of stairs together, as a team, as a rumble from the upstairs sent pieces of the house crashing to the floor. Just bits here and there, but Gemma didn't want to stick around to see how much of it would be devoured.

They pushed outside, into the safety of the yard. Gemma turned to look, doubling back at the sight of the entire top half of the house engulfed in flames.

"The fire department?"

"Too far." Matt shook his head. "I'll call to report it, but it's too late for them to save it."

For a second she'd forgotten that they were on an island.

Fear stabbed her stomach. Alone with a killer.

"Matt. He might still be here. Unless he's already gone to his boat, the killer may be here with us."

Her chest tightened. She'd thought escaping

the burning house would be the best thing that could happen. But what if he was here, watching? Waiting for the right moment? Getting out of that house and out into the open where they could be attacked at any moment might have been the most dangerous step to take.

With them out of the house and that immediate danger passed, Matt took a minute to look at Gemma's hands behind her back. The knots were good, he hadn't been able to break them, but in the light he could take his pocketknife to the ropes, and as long as he was careful, she'd be free.

"Hold still. Just one minute. I'm going to cut you free."

He heard her breathing change from normal fear to terror. Matt had to get her free and out of there fast.

"You can do it, Gemma, just let me cut..." He was careful with how he touched her broken wrist, but he could still see her body tense when his hands grazed it. The idea that someone had exploited her injury as a way to subdue and try to kill her...

Matt reminded himself to stay calm, focused for a minute on his own breathing. He needed to slow everything down, take things one step at a time, get them out of there alive.

Maybe catch whoever was behind this in the process.

He couldn't believe they'd been so close, that they'd been on the same little square of property with the guy and Matt still hadn't gotten him.

He didn't get mad often. It reminded him too much of his dad, whom he never wanted to emulate. But right now… When would this stop? When would he be able to put this to an end? The criminal behind this sure wasn't going to quit anytime soon. The more Matt thought about his behavior, about the case as a whole, the more he thought their killer was the leader of the gang behind the thefts—and the deaths. And maybe he was still leading some men. It would explain his ability to be everywhere, have eyes everywhere.

Which meant there could be more than one man here, ready for a fight on this island.

But Matt wasn't giving up.

One more good cut and Gemma's hands were free. She rubbed her hurt wrist without taking her eyes from the flames. "Thank you."

He nodded. "Let's go." He reached for her hand, determined not to let them get separated again. They ran together down the path through the woods, Matt readying himself around every curve to draw his weapon if he needed to, but knowing that taking a slower path through the woods was just as dangerous in this situation. Time wasn't on their side.

They raced to where he'd tied up the kayaks, came out of the narrow woods path onto a beach where there was…

Nothing. The boats were gone.

Matt squinted. Saw one kayak two hundred yards or so out, being carried away by the ocean current. The other was in the opposite direction, in the marsh, so the current wasn't carrying it.

It was being rowed.

So Gemma's attacker had escaped. Taken their boats and done who knew what with whatever transport he'd taken to get there. And left them on an island to die.

Because if the house fire didn't get put out soon, the entire island could go up in flames.

Please let it rain, Matt prayed with all his heart. And thunder rumbled.

But the skies, the ground, stayed dry.

"We have to do something!" Gemma yelled, tears now streaming down her face.

Matt reached for his phone. Service out here was sketchy at best, but maybe…

"Hello?"

"Chief, it's O'Dell. I'm out on Whitetail Island with Gemma. The man we're after was here, but he got away. We are trapped on the island with no boats and there's a large house fire." He delivered the information as quickly as he could.

"We'll send someone out to get you both. Water's choppy around here with the storm, but it shouldn't take too long. Hang tight and try to keep her calm."

"I will," Matt promised.

"Matt!" Gemma's voice was more insistent. He turned to her, kept the phone at his ear.

"Tell him that there's a room in the house— though it's probably burned by now. But there were maps. Maps of places I've been. Pictures of me around town."

He shivered. Calling the man a stalker had been more accurate than he'd realized. Matt nodded. "Sir? Gemma just told me there's a room in the house with maps of her whereabouts. The man truly has been stalking her, and it appears this may have been serving as a sort of command center."

"Then, we'd better hope the fire doesn't destroy everything we could have used as evidence. Because we need to catch him. It appears this man isn't giving up. As many close calls as we've had, I'm afraid we're running out of chances. One of these times…" The chief's voice trailed off.

Matt looked away from Gemma, couldn't handle being pulled into her dark eyes and seeing the way she looked at him, like he could keep her safe, like she trusted him to. Instead, he focused on the dark plume of smoke rising in the distance, tried to remind himself that no matter how his feelings had gotten involved, this was still a case. And he was good at his job. He could do it. Prove himself.

"I know, sir," he confirmed.

"I'm counting on you."

"Yes, Chief."

And they hung up the phone.

"There's so much smoke."

Too much, Matt feared, to hope that they'd be able to investigate any of what Gemma had seen in that room. It was likely gone. Once again, they only had her memory as evidence.

He looked over at her, tried to put himself in her shoes. What was it like to carry the weight of the knowledge she had for a decade? To truly believe that someone had been murdered but to have no evidence to substantiate her claims? To wonder if someone had gone free because no one believed her?

And then to find out all these years later that she was right.

"I'm sorry, Gemma."

She turned to him, face streaked with tears. "You got us out. That was all you could do."

"I don't mean that. I mean, everything. I'm sorry you've had to go through all this, that this nightmare has lasted so long."

"It is what it is." Gemma's shoulders fell as she looked back at the smoke.

"Who do you think is doing this?"

"It's hard to imagine anyone in Treasure Point acting like this. Whoever it is, I don't think they know me."

"They stalk you awfully well. Doesn't that seem to contradict that thought?"

Gemma shook her head. "I don't think so. I still think it's someone from a nearby town."

Matt didn't argue with her. She didn't seem emotionally ready to consider the possibility that her attacker could be someone she knew.

"His laugh." Gemma said the words out of the blue, catching Matt off guard.

"His laugh?"

She nodded. "I would recognize it. I don't know why I wasn't able to place the voice a decade ago, even though it seemed familiar to me. But if I heard it again, I'm sure I'd know that laugh."

"Wait, if you recognized his voice years ago, what makes you think he wouldn't be from Treasure Point?"

"I got out of town a decent amount back then. I spent a summer or two working on St. Simons and I was taking a college class in the afternoons in Savannah. It still doesn't mean anything."

Matt dropped that line of questioning. Pursuing it wasn't getting them anywhere right now.

Instead, he watched the smoke, waited for rescue and tried to figure out what lead to pursue next. They needed to know who wanted to see Gemma killed before he or she succeeded.

THIRTEEN

Less than ten minutes had passed since Matt's phone call with the chief when the rescue boat arrived. As they climbed in, Gemma let out a sigh of relief.

"Close call," commented Clay, who was driving the boat. "I looked for anyone suspicious in the marsh on my way, but didn't see anyone or anything. No one at the dock in Treasure Point had seen anything, either."

"Was there anyone you didn't recognize at the boat dock?"

Clay shook his head. "Sorry, just town regulars." As he spoke, he maneuvered the boat away from the island and out into the water. "The chief wants to see you both at the station. I'll give you a ride there after we dock."

Gemma had seen that coming. It still didn't make it less intimidating, though, walking into the police station for the first time in over a decade.

By the time they'd finally gotten there, she still hadn't managed to convince herself to be less intimidated. But she took a deep breath and followed Matt in anyway.

"O'Dell. Miss Phillips. Have a seat, I want to hear what happened." The chief wasted no time with pleasantries, something Gemma could appreciate.

"Sir, I charted out the addresses of homes that had maps stolen in the case Gemma testified in a decade ago, and today I planned to drive out to all of them and see if I could figure out any pattern to the places that were hit. I thought it might give us an indication of who could be behind all of this, or maybe even help us predict the next place that might be hit."

"And one of those places was the house on Whitetail Island. I see."

Silence hovered for just a minute. A thick, heavy silence that could burst any minute into a storm of words that Gemma didn't need to hear. Matt had been as vague as possible with her earlier when describing what had happened on that island years before. Though the case had remained unsolved and eventually turned cold, there were plenty of details, enough to give a person nightmares for weeks. That house... It was good that it had burned.

He hated that greed led people to spill blood like that.

"When we arrived there," Matt continued, "we decided to investigate the house itself a little, since I knew it had been…involved to a greater degree than some of the others. I was in the back looking in an outbuilding and called to Gemma to join me. Too many minutes passed and I wondered if she'd gotten stuck on some of the thorns in the overgrowth. And then I smelled smoke."

"And what was happening to you?"

Gemma recounted her experience, which was about what Matt had assumed from how her hands were tied. Her stalker had tied her up, tossed her in a room and left her for dead once he'd started that fire. Destroying the evidence of his "command center" and his only witness all in one light of a match? Brilliant.

And pure, coldhearted evil.

"Miss Phillips," the chief began once they were done filling him in, "do you have any idea who could be behind the threats against you?"

She glanced at Matt. "Matt asked me the same thing earlier. I'm afraid I don't, sir. I suppose it could be someone from around town, although I doubt it. My best guesses are that it is someone from Savannah or St. Simons, because I don't think it's someone I know from Treasure Point."

"Someone is stalking you because you were a witness in this case. Remind me why it's necessary that they know you outside that?"

"Because I recognized the voice, sir. I couldn't place it, but it was definitely familiar. I spent enough time in Savannah and St. Simons that year that it could have been someone I knew from one of those places."

"What voice?"

Gemma frowned. "When I heard the men arguing in the woods ten years ago." She glanced at Matt, but he looked as confused as she did. "I had run from the first men—the ones I saw hiding the things they'd stolen. But then I tripped, and when I went to get up, I could hear an argument. I could only see one of them, Harris, who ended up dead. The other man, the one who sounded angry, I couldn't see, but I could hear him. His voice sounded familiar, but I couldn't identify it. I told the police officers at the time, but they didn't seem to think it was important. And even though Harris had disappeared, since there was no evidence that foul play had been involved in his disappearance, and I couldn't place the man's voice...basically I was told that no one believed me, that I must have gotten mixed up after the trauma of knowing I was seeing people cover up a crime."

"I was never told any of this." The chief shook his head. "Generally on cases like this, one officer has the lead and the chief receives updates. Your story must have seemed insignificant to whoever was briefing me at the time."

"It doesn't seem insignificant now, though. Essentially Gemma knew this murder took place a decade ago. And that one of the men from the crime ring was still walking free."

The chief's frown deepened. "And you knew this?"

"Not until she told me last week." Matt shook his head.

"This is the first I'm hearing of any of it. Go to Savannah today, St. Simons, too, if you have time. Make a whole reunion kind of trip out of it and see if you turn up any leads. We need something on this, O'Dell. Fast."

As though he didn't know it. "I'm working on it, sir."

The chief glanced at Gemma. Opened his mouth. Closed it and shook his head.

Matt knew all the things the chief wanted to stay, statistics about how time was against them, how they could only avoid Gemma falling victim to one of these attacks for so long. He knew, and he was helpless to do anything about it. He couldn't solve the case until he had the pieces necessary to do so and right now he didn't.

Matt needed them. Yesterday. "I know, sir," he said to the chief as Gemma looked back and forth between the two of them, the look on her face perplexed and curious.

"All right. Go see what you can get. I'd like a report tomorrow. I want to stay on top of the case this time—not to micromanage you, O'Dell. You've done a good job so far. A real good job. But…"

"I get that, too." The chief couldn't afford to let anything go without his notice this time. Because last time it had cost them ten years of a killer roaming free, close to their safe little town or even in it.

If anyone else died, Matt realized then, the chief and Matt were both going to blame themselves.

No one could die. No one else. This ended now.

"Ready, Gemma?" Matt stood. It would take less than an hour to get where they needed to go, and it was going to take all the self-restraint in him not to burn up the road at a faster speed than was safe.

"I'm ready."

They left the office together, said nothing on the walk to the car and climbed in.

As soon as the doors had shut, Gemma turned to him. "The chief is afraid he's going to get me, isn't he?"

Matt clenched and unclenched his jaw. He wasn't ready to have this conversation. Wouldn't ever be ready. "We don't need to talk about this now."

"But we do. If we don't find something…" She brushed a tear from her cheek. Sighed heavily as if she was irritated that it would dare fall, ruin the mask of indifference she usually liked to keep on her face to cover the range of emotions hidden there. "The idea of losing my life, of these twenty-eight years being all I get, that's hard enough. If I die before we finish this case? Then this Gemma is all people will ever know. They'll never separate me from this case. And I won't be around to deal with that, but my family will. My parents, my sister, will know that not only did I always remain the odd one out, the one who was 'adopted,' not the real Phillips, but I also had to live my adult years completely defined by someone else's crime. I never became the person they wanted me to be—someone they could be proud of."

Matt had been about to put the car in Drive,

get out of the parking lot and out of town. But this needed to be dealt with first.

He faced her. Full on. She still looked down at her lap. Embarrassed about the words she'd just said? "Look at me, Gemma."

She wouldn't. Didn't.

"Please."

Still no response. Matt reached over, slowly placed his hand underneath her chin, moved it ever so slightly up and toward him. "Is that what this is about? Why you feel like you have to try so hard to prove that you are more than this case? To make your family proud?"

He hadn't been adopted. Didn't know what that was like, although some days he wondered if it would have been better if he had been. But he knew when one more tear slipped down her cheek, followed by a nod, that he'd finally understood.

They *both* just wanted to be known for who they had been. They wanted the opportunity to be able to be proud of who they were.

And maybe that was why he'd always felt connected to her.

"Maybe that is it. Even if it is, is that so bad?"

Matt didn't know.

The drive to St. Simons went by quickly. The two of them spent the next hour chasing down people on the island that Gemma had known the summer she worked there, pretending to be visiting for the fun of it. None of their voices sounded to Gemma like the man who was after her. They did the same thing in Savannah.

Still nothing.

"I know you were hoping to find something." Matt's voice had just the right amount of empathy. Somehow it helped ease Gemma's disappointment, at least a little.

Gemma exhaled. "Somehow I thought it would break tonight. Silly, right? Why today?"

"Hey, but why not? It could have. And soon, it will."

She wished she could be that sure.

"Let's head back to Treasure Point," she said at the same time that he said, "We might as well find somewhere here to have a late dinner."

Gemma looked over at him. "You need to rest. You can't work this case every hour of the day or you'll burn out before it's over."

His expression admitted that she was right, even if his words didn't. And somehow she'd thought that would be the end of it, that they'd climb into the car and head back to their little town, get some sleep and try harder tomorrow.

"I do need rest," Matt said slowly. "Both of us do. So I think dinner in Savannah is a great idea. We'll take an hour or two to eat and try to give our minds a rest, then go home, sleep and get at the case tomorrow."

"But…" She didn't know why she was protesting. They both had to eat, she was hungry and everything he said made sense.

Except…an hour or two in Savannah with him, without the case as a buffer? Walking down River Street at night with the city lights reflecting off the water, mystery and romance dancing in the air in every dangling strand of Spanish moss? How was she supposed to handle something like that?

Gemma was about to protest again when Matt took her hand. Funny, it felt like friendship when he held it tight like that. Even though so much of what passed between them felt like more, felt deeper than anything she'd shared with anyone, holding his hand didn't give her butterflies, per se. It just felt…

Right.

They walked away from the parking lot, across a square and underneath the towering oak trees whose branches arched over the sidewalks, until they reached a stone staircase that would take them down to River Street and dinner.

"What's your favorite shop down here?" he asked when they'd reached the bottom.

No hesitation on her part. "The candy store."

"River Street Sweets?"

Gemma nodded. "That's the one. You go in and just *smell*. I'm pretty sure the mere act of sniffing in there can make a person gain five or ten pounds, but it's worth it."

"Let's go there first, then."

"Matt. Dinner?" She gave him a scolding look, but inside she was smiling.

"We'll get there eventually. Don't rush, just enjoy it."

Was it just dinner he was talking about? Or the way their friendship seemed slowly to be turning into something more, something deeper?

They made their way down the sidewalk, passing one man who was playing the saxophone and another who was selling roses made out of palm fronds. "I always thought those were so cool," Gemma commented once they'd passed the man with the flowers. The words were halfway out of her mouth before it occurred to her that they sounded like a hint, and she corrected herself as soon as she caught it. "No, I didn't—"

But Matt was already paying the man and reaching for a rose. "I wanted to."

He smiled as he handed it to her, and she took it from him. "Thank you."

They came to the candy store then, stepped

up the stone step that led them inside the brightly lit shop, and Gemma stopped just inside the door as she always did, took a deep breath. "Smells like my childhood."

"You came here often?"

Gemma nodded. "My parents would bring us here, oh, every few months. They love the city and they wanted us to experience it. My grandparents live here, and a lot of my extended family, too."

"Nice. So where should we eat? Your choice."

"Let's go to The Pirates' House." You couldn't go wrong with the classic River Street restaurant.

They picked out a few pieces of candy, paid for them and walked toward the restaurant. Dinner was perfect as far as Gemma was concerned. They talked, laughed, and Gemma wondered how she'd gone so many years without Matt in her life. He seemed like such a natural part of it now.

When dinner was over they started walking again, deciding without talking about it to head down as close to the water as they could get. The night grew darker, the city sounds were joined by a cadence of crickets at the water's edge, and the two of them just stood there. Listening.

Time kept going. Minutes? Hours? Gemma

didn't know. All she knew was that they were there, together without saying a word, without anything touching except their hands, and everything felt like it should.

"What time is it? We should head back before it's too late." After all that had happened, Claire would be sure to rally the cavalry if Gemma was home a second after midnight—the curfew they'd agreed on.

"It's ten."

Not nearly as late as she would have guessed. Funny how long you could stand in silence with someone and find it to be one of the best parts of your day, when it was the right person.

"So…back to town?"

"If you want to."

Gemma wasn't sure, didn't know what she wanted. Standing there with Matt…yes, she wanted that. But what about her family? All she wanted was for them to be proud, for them to be happy they'd picked her to add to their family. She wanted them to approve of the choices she'd made—including who she chose to spend her life with.

Well, that was not *all* she wanted. She wanted a family of her own one day, little kids to raise with a husband she loved.

"We can stay a little while longer." She said the words with her heart pounding, every emotion within her questioning the decisions she was making right now.

"Then, let's walk some more." He took her hand and they wandered River Street until they'd seen everything. "Want to see one of my favorite spots in the city?" he asked her in a voice that sent chills to her toes with its softness. Gemma nodded.

Matt led her back up the stone steps to downtown and they walked for several blocks. "This is it," he said when they were standing in the middle of a square. He looked down at her, eyes searching hers as if he was looking for some sort of reaction. Gemma looked around. At first glance nothing made this square—Oglethorpe Square—any different from many of the others. But when she looked closer, she saw many things she liked…the shell of an old theater over on one side, a cute coffee shop on another, and the whole thing overhung by thick branches of live oak trees that tangled overtop of them, draped by Spanish moss that reflected the orange glow of the streetlights on its edges.

She looked back at him.

And knew that square, in a way, was like Matt. An everyday guy, maybe not as obviously romantic as some…but special, if you took the time to notice.

She looked up to tell him she loved it, that

she saw the square like he did, but when she moved her face toward him, he moved his down, put his hands on either side of her face and pressed his lips to hers.

And what a kiss.

Seconds passed slowly. Gemma forgot about the case, forgot about her mixed feelings about returning to Treasure Point, forgot about everything except the feeling of their lips together, the slight roughness of his five-o'clock shadow brushing her cheek.

Matt pulled away first. "Wow."

"I know."

"Gemma…" Matt ran a hand through his hair, walked a few feet away, then back. "I don't know what to do."

"Me, neither."

More silence. More pacing.

"We don't have to decide anything yet," Gemma said, feeling as if she needed the reminder as much as he did. "We can just…be whatever we are. Who we are."

He didn't kiss her this time. Instead, he wrapped his arms around her, pulling her in for a hug that made her feel safe.

Loved?

And then they drove back to Treasure Point in the darkness, Gemma alternating between nodding off in the passenger seat and wondering how this relationship was going to work. She wanted to believe they'd both be happy, but with the nightmare dinner with her parents still in the forefront of her mind, she couldn't help but wonder if the two of them being together was doomed from the start. And which of them would be hurt more if it all imploded.

FOURTEEN

Gemma leaned back in her chair the next morning at work and smiled—not just because of her date with Matt the night before, but because of the work she'd gotten done so far today. Finally, she was making some progress. Her initial list of ideas for the museum was a good one, but she'd been able to expand it even further. They actually had a chance to make this work; Gemma could feel it.

Jim Howard sat across from her in the portable office building, reading over her list of ideas to get the townspeople themselves invested in the museum. She bit her lip—a tick she hated on other people and rarely resorted to—as she waited. It was important to her that this worked, not just because she wanted the town and her parents to be proud of the job she'd done, but because she cared. About the museum, about this little town, about all of them being able to move on from the danger hanging over them and be brought back together helping the town they all loved.

Jim looked up at her. Smiled for the first time she could remember. "It looks perfect, Gemma. These are workable ideas and I think...I think maybe this place has a chance after all."

She smiled. "I'm glad you think so."

"Good work. You should be very proud. We certainly are. The historical society has decided—unanimously—to drop the trial period. The job is yours, Gemma."

"Unanimously?"

Jim chuckled. "Even Cindy Anne liked your new plans. Though she probably won't admit it." He nodded his approval, picked up the papers she'd given him and walked out.

Half an hour later Gemma decided to duck out a little early. Maybe she'd call Matt, tell him about what the head of the historical society had said, see if he wanted to celebrate with her. She felt a little bit of blush rise to her cheeks at the thought of Matt. Calling him? Dating him?

Who would have thought?

Yet it was perfect, just like her ideas for the museum had turned out to be. Surprisingly simple, the two of them being reunited and pursuing what had started out as a hint of high school attraction. Simple but beautiful.

Gemma was most of the way to her car when

she spotted something…odd. Something was on the windshield, and while her first thought was to wonder whether Matt had left something for her, her second thought was more defensive.

She moved closer cautiously, unable to decide if she should leave whatever it was alone entirely and wait for Matt or another officer to check it out, or if she should give in to curiosity and see for herself.

Gemma moved closer. Within five feet of the car she finally identified the dark shape as black roses. She squinted. Not just black roses. Black palm roses, a painted version of the ones sold in Savannah. Beside them was a note, typed in nondescript large type.

HOPE YOU HAD A GOOD LAST TRIP TO RIVER STREET. DID YOU SEE ME THERE, WATCHING YOU?

Gemma wanted to throw up. The idea that he'd been so close last night…he must have been waiting for an opportunity to snatch her, but something had told her not to leave Matt's side, so she hadn't, not for the whole time they'd been out of Treasure Point.

That instinct had saved her life. At least for now.

She dialed Matt's number, backed away from the car.

It didn't take long for Matt to make it to the scene—he'd been on the other side of the Hamilton Estate, investigating a tip one of the construction workers had given him. Gemma frowned. Had it been a legitimate tip? Or were the construction workers—who she'd pretty much overlooked on the suspect list—more of a threat than she had thought?

Shiloh was with Matt, dressed in her crime scene uniform. She slid gloves into place, then approached the flowers.

"You found them just like this? You didn't touch them, right?" Shiloh directed the question to Gemma.

Gemma shook her head. "No. I didn't touch any of it."

"Good." Shiloh picked the arrangement up carefully, slowly examining all sides of it as she lifted it off the hood of the car.

Then she dropped it back down. "There's something in that."

"You want me to get gloves and pick it up?"

Shiloh glared at him. "If I thought someone should pick it up, I would do it myself."

Gemma almost snickered. This woman was something else.

They all waited, crowding closer around—

and watched as a scorpion crawled from somewhere in the middle of the tight bunch of palm flowers. Gemma was used to scorpions found in Georgia, a darker brown variety that wasn't terribly poisonous. This one was light tan, almost translucent, and the sight of it sent shivers up her spine.

"We have to catch him." Matt looked around, the options for catching a scorpion limited at a construction site with only a few cars and a portable office building to go to for materials.

"I've got an empty coffee cup in my car." Shiloh was already moving that way. She returned with it seconds later and Matt scooted the paper cup along next to the scorpion, holding his breath as he used the lid to sweep it in, then closed the lid tight.

Everyone seemed to exhale at once.

"He tried to kill me again." Gemma stated the obvious in a quivering voice. She'd been proud of herself most of this whole time for how she'd handled the situation, staying strong and determined to catch the killer no matter what it took. It was inevitable, though, that she'd start to break eventually. They had to solve this fast, before she fell apart completely.

Another car pulled in as Matt was putting a piece of tape over the drinking hole on the coffee cup—no chance that guy was getting out. A little more tension eased from Gemma's shoulders.

The chief climbed out of the car and walked toward Matt. "What's going on? I heard you call units here on the radio."

Matt gave him a rundown of the situation.

The chief nodded. "All right. I want someone with Gemma at all times. This guy's getting desperate. Matt, I want you to come with me to the station. Let's see if we can get an ID on this guy and piece together an idea of how this could have happened."

Matt looked at Gemma. Torn.

She nodded. "I'll be okay." He needed to go. She'd be fine with another officer, just as long as someone was watching her. Or at least she *thought* she would be—but as she watched Matt drive away in his patrol car, part of her felt a little less strong, a little less brave than she had just moments before.

After Matt, the chief, Shiloh and the other officers headed out, it was just a few construction workers left working at the museum site and Clay, who was going to give Gemma a ride home. She just needed a few more minutes in the office to grab her purse and her things, and then she was going to leave, too. She hurried up the stairs, and back inside the building.

Her phone rang just as she got inside. Matt. "Hello?"

"They think they ID'd the type of scorpion. It looks like an Arizona bark scorpion. Not just a threat—that one's deadly."

"We're in Georgia. Someone went to the trouble to get a scorpion here from Arizona? How? Why?"

"Mailed it, I would guess. As far as why, if you'd picked up that bouquet and held it for even a few seconds, he probably would have stung you—and then crawled away, leaving little to no evidence about who was behind it. That's easier than killing you himself."

Gemma understood. It was sick. But it made sense. The man who was after her was getting more desperate to get her out of the picture, getting more creative and determined by the second. She shivered. "I've got to go, Matt. I'll talk to you later, but I want to get out of here."

"All right. You're okay with Clay, right? The chief wanted me to be part of this."

She nodded even though he couldn't see her. "Clay's waiting for me just outside. I'm fine. Talk to you soon."

They hung up and Gemma rubbed her arms to try to make the goose bumps go away. Time to gather her things and then she could go. She walked farther into the room, looked around to make sure she was getting everything she'd brought with her this morning.

She paused at the desk, noticing a small folded piece of paper. She'd almost gotten it unfolded when all at once, alarm bells in her brain sounded.

If he had been here *since* leaving the palm flowers, he was probably still here. And he wanted her dead. Today.

Gemma dropped to her knees just as the first gunshot pierced the window on the other side of where she'd been standing.

She'd been right. The note had been a trap, a reason for her to stand still in the killer's line of sight. She crawled toward the door but stayed low. More gunshots outside. She knew some would belong to the killer, some to Clay, who would be shooting back as long as he had eyes on his target.

This had to end soon.

Hands shaking, she unfolded the note, not ready to read it, but knowing there could be something in it she needed to know.

TOMORROW MORNING. HAMIL-TON ESTATE WHERE THE HAUL WAS BURIED. COME ALONE AND BE READY TO TELL ME WHAT YOU'VE TOLD THE COPS.

As this went on, he was seeming less stable. Gemma couldn't take much more of this. She shoved the note in her pocket, curled up against the wall and waited for the shooting to stop.

Then she heard someone shouting outside the door. "Gemma, it's Clay. He's stopped for now, let's go."

Running to the car not knowing if the shooting would start again sounded dangerous. Then again, the paper-thin walls of the portable office building weren't exactly offering a lot of protection.

Clay cracked the door open and they ran to the patrol car. Nothing. Not a shot fired. Trying to figure out this guy's motives, staying one step ahead of him, was getting nearly impossible.

They drove to Claire's house without talking. There was nothing to say. And Gemma didn't want to share the contents of this note with anyone but Matt.

Just to make this nightmare end sooner, she was half considering doing what it asked.

"I need to see you in my office."

The chief's voice was more businesslike than Matt had heard it in a while, understandable with the new threat against Gemma earlier today. In fact, its tone was so different from usual that he half questioned the handful of interactions they'd had over the past weeks. Hadn't it just been yesterday that the chief had given him what had amounted to a pep talk, let him know that he thought he could handle this case?

Now…things were falling apart. Matt could feel it, tried to brace himself for it, but he still wasn't ready when it came.

"You're off the case, O'Dell." The words fell like a gavel—and Matt could feel the accompanying judgment—the moment he had shut the door behind himself.

"Off the… Sir, why? I've been doing the best I can, and I really think I'm getting closer to finding this guy. I know you wanted it solved as quickly as possible, but I don't think you're going to find anyone who will work it with half the determination I will." He fought for it, not sure if he stood any chance at all, but figuring it couldn't hurt.

"Frankly, I'm uncomfortable with how close you are to this case."

Unbelievable.

"Chief, you're the one who reminded me less than a week ago that my dad and I are different people. His crimes are in the past and don't affect this at all."

A funny expression crossed his face, but he

shook it off. "We'll talk about that in a minute. For now, it's not your father I was referring to."

Matt all but fell backward into the chair he'd been standing in front of. He kept staring at the chief, even as the pieces started to fit, as the conversation started to seem less crazy and began making sense. "Gemma."

"Yes."

"But we aren't… I mean, I don't know…and why do you think there's something going on anyway?"

"Her parents came to talk to me."

Stunned fell short of explaining how he felt right now. "Her parents…but…" He searched for what he wanted to say, wanted to ask. Every fiber of him wanted to stand up, be a man, defend himself.

But he'd been getting romantically involved with a witness in a case he was investigating.

There was no way to spin that, no way to make it sound better than it was. Because Matt should have known better. *Had* known better. But his feelings for Gemma had been so strong that he'd ignored the conflict of interest, or at least minimized it in his mind, to make it seem possible for them to be together.

The thing was, he still wasn't sure he completely regretted it. Matt's only option here was full honesty. He'd plead his case and see what happened.

"Sir, if you've heard that I'm emotionally involved with Gemma, then I suspect that what you heard is true. And I…I'm apologetic that my choices reflect badly on the department. I should have known better."

"Yes, you should have."

He didn't know what to say to that.

A few seconds passed. Finally, he had one more thought. "Sir, if I can say so, this is still not affecting my work on the case in a negative way. If I thought for a second that it was, I would fully understand your choice to have me taken off it. But it's not. I'm still the best man to work this case."

The chief shook his head. "I'm sorry, O'Dell, but I can't take the risk of an emotional response compromising the case. Besides, if it comes down to it, we may have to use Gemma's presence to draw her stalker in closer."

Matt was up on his feet, all but in the chief's face faster than he could blink. "You can't do that."

"That's exactly what a man who is too close to the situation would say." The older man kept his voice steady, level. Certain.

Matt sat back down.

"Even if this wasn't an issue, there's a bigger

problem with you continuing to be involved. Your father... He seems to have escaped from prison."

Matt shook his head. "Why does that matter? You said yourself that I wasn't responsible for his mistakes. I haven't heard from him, nothing like that in case you're wondering."

"I know. You're a good cop, O'Dell. I don't doubt your loyalties at all."

"But you're taking me off this case."

The chief leaned back in his chair, rubbed his temples with both hands. "I don't have any choice. You're off the case for now and I'm going to have you...take some time off. Take a break, refocus. If you can lie low for a week or two, just until this resolves, which hopefully won't take any longer, you'll still have a job when you come back."

"And if not?"

He shook his head. "I'm not the only one watching, O'Dell. The Phillips family has a lot of influence in this town. I've got the mayor, town council members breathing down my neck. You mess this up? I may not be able to guarantee your place here at the Treasure Point Police Department."

Matt didn't say another word. Just stood and walked out of the office, straight to his car. He jammed the keys in the ignition, started the engine and headed straight for Gemma's house even as everything inside him screamed that it was a bad idea. He should go home, think about it.

But he'd done something wrong. He hadn't been the man he wanted to be. Dating a witness? He shook his head at himself, at his selfishness. Gemma was too good for him anyway; everyone knew it. He was practically taking advantage of the chaos the whole situation had plunged her life into. And that was the last thing he wanted to do. That meant he needed to take a big step back—and before he could, he owed her an explanation.

He pulled into the driveway, took a deep breath and got out of the car.

Gemma must have seen him pull up, because she walked onto the front porch and out to the driveway, dressed in a Georgia football fitted T-shirt and jeans.

She looked good.

"Hey." Her smile was sweet, soft.

And he was about to be the one to take it away. Matt shook his head to shake himself out of it. It had to be done.

"We need to talk."

The smile fell away. "Okay."

"I'm off the case, Gemma. I'm sorry, but I can't do anything about it. So, uh…I guess this is goodbye. I know they'll solve it soon, you'll be able to get back to Atlanta…" Matt cleared his throat, tried to talk past the lump forming in his throat.

"Wait, what do you mean, off the case? And why are you telling me goodbye?"

Clear brown eyes met his, and while usually he loved looking into her eyes, feeling the odd but welcome sense of a connection with her, today it was uncomfortable. Too close.

Matt looked away. Shook his head. "I'm sorry. Another officer will be guarding your house." He motioned to the unmarked car sitting on the street two houses down. "Goodbye, Gemma."

"No." She stepped down off the porch onto the driveway, feeling fire start to burn in her chest. She took a deep breath, let it out again.

"No?"

She repeated herself one more time, this time shaking her head slowly to go along with the one word. "No."

He leaned against his car, folded his arms and looked her way. His expression was different than it had been the entire rest of the time they'd been working on this case together. It was guarded, harder.

But Gemma knew the real Matt now.

"I think you're running."

"Excuse me?"

"You're running, Matt, from the slightest hint of trouble. We knew, you and I both did, that being…friends, being whatever we are wasn't going to be easy. And now there's trouble and you're just going to quit?"

"I didn't have the best role models about relationships, okay? Maybe you're right, maybe that is what I'm doing." He shoved a hand through his hair, an action Gemma had noticed him doing maybe once before when he was overwhelmingly frustrated. "But it's my choice."

Gemma shrugged, tried to hold back the tears she could feel threatening to spill over any second now. "Fine, if that's what you want. It's what I would have expected from the Matt I knew in high school, but I thought the man you are now was different."

He leveled his gaze at her. "You want to talk about running away?"

She swallowed hard, looked away.

"You ran first. You're fighting this battle because you know you have to in order to stay alive. But if you could, you'd have run again, wouldn't you? Just like you did before when you tried to bury yourself under a bunch of fancy clothes and a big Atlanta corporation, as if that was the way to prove you were better than this town. Didn't stop you from coming back, though, did it?"

"Me leaving was something I had to do. So was coming back." Now it was her turn to add an edge to her tone. How dare he turn this around to her?

"You want to know why I think that is, since we're analyzing each other here?"

She didn't. And she did. And he was going to tell her anyway, she could tell by the look on his face, so she stayed quiet and waited.

"I think you're afraid to let the past go. You're afraid to be any other version of Gemma than the one who had bad things happen to her. You *want* the past to define you, because otherwise you have to find a way to move on, grow."

Anything she might have prepared herself for would have been easier to handle than that. She felt the sting of the words all the way to her core, but...

Was he wrong?

Before she could respond, he shook his head. "I'm sorry, Gemma. Even if we aren't... We can't... No matter what our relationship is or isn't, I should never have talked to you like that. I'm truly sorry." He was back in his car and gone before she could say another word. Before she could tell him that maybe he was right, or tell him about the letter she'd received earlier.

Her only comfort was that he'd driven away before he could see her break down and cry.

Likely the first of many tears to come.

FIFTEEN

Gemma had been left almost speechless after the conversation with Matt. She wasn't mad, not really. What he'd said about her…it may have been true. She wasn't sure yet. And in any case, she couldn't blame him for snapping at her when every word she'd heard him say was covered in hurt, insecurity.

She was almost sure he'd go straight from her house to their beach near the Hamilton House to try to sort out his thoughts. Unfortunately, this time she doubted that a few hours in the fresh air would make things better. This was too complicated for that.

As for herself, she skipped dinner. Cried over the past, over their shared hurts, over the unendingness of this case, over losing Matt. Cried until there weren't any tears left.

And then fell asleep.

Claire opened the shop late the next morning so she could make chocolate-chip muffins for Gemma.

"I'm so sorry," her sister repeated for the millionth time as the two of them sat cross-legged beside each other on the couch.

"It's not your fault."

This time Claire argued. "But it is, Gemma. I saw you two kiss, when you'd hurt your wrist. I told Mom and Dad that you were working with him on this case and also getting romantically involved."

Okay, awkward, but still not something she could see as directly leading to their...breakup, or whatever you called something like that when you hadn't technically been dating in the first place.

"Still, don't blame yourself, Claire. I don't even know what happened."

"But I do. That's what I'm trying to tell you." Claire uncrossed her legs, leaned forward in her spot on the couch. "I told them and they said they would go and talk to the chief."

"The chief? What does he have to do with anything?"

Her sister shifted again. "Nothing. He shouldn't have anything to do with your and Matt's relationship. But Mom and Dad figured... They knew..."

"They knew that if they pointed out to the

chief that the officer in charge of my investigation might be dating me, Matt would lose his job."

Claire nodded. "Yeah."

So it had been intentional. Gemma debated how much she should let it bother her. On one hand, her parents had been so far out of line to bring something so personal to the attention of Matt's boss. On the other, maybe she and Matt had been crazy to think they could start a relationship while in the situation they were in without consequences.

The whole idea had been doomed from the beginning. That first time she'd seen him again, when she'd been interviewing for the job and he'd walked across the parking lot, she should have looked away and never looked back.

But if she had it to do over again, she'd do exactly the same thing. Gemma wiped a tear from her cheek. Being with Matt, getting closer to him the way she had, had been worth it. Was *still* worth it.

"Thanks for telling me." She finally found the words to tell Claire.

Her sister gave her a small smile. "I have to get to work."

"Yes, go, I'll be fine." Gemma continued drinking her coffee, looking up to wave to her sister as she started to walk out the door.

"Gemma, I like Matt now. I really do. And I'm sorry for saying anything to them."

"You didn't mean for this to happen."

Claire smiled. "Love you. I'm glad we're sisters."

She waved and then she was gone. Sisters. Never once had Claire treated her like anything but her real, true sister. For that matter, her parents had never treated her like anything but their real, true daughter. Why, then, did Gemma feel like the adoption was so often at the forefront of her own mind, factoring into her own thoughts?

Maybe it shouldn't be. She didn't know.

Gemma had mostly forgiven Matt. Really, she had. She'd forgiven him for kissing her back the time she'd initiated that incredible, beyond-words kiss. She'd forgiven him for convincing her they didn't need to consider the practicality of a relationship between the two of them.

What she was struggling with was forgiving him for abandoning her. Last she knew, he was questioning how much they should see each other, and then he was just…gone. Not helping her with the case, not answering her calls this morning.

So today she was ending this. Not the investigation, although that would be nice, too—she was ending this standoff with Matt. If he'd decided they shouldn't date…fine.

Even if it did make her feel like someone had tossed her heart to the alligators in some backwoods creek.

But to refuse to accept her help with the case? He needed her. She was about to show him that.

Gemma dialed his number one more time. He still didn't answer. She grabbed her purse, hurried outside to the car. She hadn't been able to sleep last night, so she'd spent her time thinking about the case. Nothing had turned up in St. Simons or Savannah, visiting places she'd frequented a decade ago. As much as Gemma hated the thought, maybe the head of the group of criminals really *was* from Treasure Point, hiding in plain sight somewhere.

The only way she knew to find him, the only hope she thought she had, was to make this meeting in the woods. The note had instructed her to meet him where she'd seen their group burying their stash all those years ago. Instead, Gemma planned to wait long enough that he should already be there, then sneak around in the woods just long enough to get a glimpse and figure out *who* they were after.

The more she thought about it, the more she was afraid it was going to be someone she knew. And the more she let herself accept that thought, the more she could almost recall who the voice had belonged to…

Her heartbeat stayed steady as she drove down the road to the Hamilton Estate. Up until she was three or four miles away.

Then a lump formed so large in her throat that for half a second, she thought she wouldn't be able to breathe. Gemma pulled over. Breathed in and out. She couldn't let fear control her. She had to do this—had to find out who was behind the threat to her life. This was the best chance she had.

Yet even after she calmed herself down, it seemed unwise.

This was a bad idea.

She wasn't going to follow through. She wanted to. She wanted to have this be over, to have her life back, to show the town who she was.

But so much of her life had been defined by one night when she was in the wrong place at the wrong time. That had been pure, awful co-incidence. Today? She'd be putting herself into that situation.

And there was no reason for her to take this into her own hands. She'd turn around in the gravel driveway just before the Hamilton Estate. She wasn't even going to set foot on that property today.

Gemma took a deep breath, rounded the last curve, saw that there was road construction. Chills crept their way down her arms, down her back. Was it legitimate, or was this like in the movies, where it was a setup?

She wasn't waiting around to find out. She backed up, prepared for a three-point or four-point or however many points it took turn, but on her second try, she ran straight into the mailman. She let out a heavy sigh, prepared to get out of the truck and apologize to Phil.

But he was getting out of his truck. And coming toward her. He looked much, much angrier than a little fender bender like this merited.

Then his anger turned to a grin. One without a hint of friendliness, just all teeth and glaring.

And then he laughed. Low. Evil.

Gemma jammed the car out of Park, into Reverse, only to find that while she'd been watching Phil approach, one of the construction trucks had pulled in behind her. Blocking her in. Making a face-to-face confrontation the only chance she had to escape…or, more than likely, the last thing she'd ever do.

She threw the door open anyway, tried to run.

But ran straight into a construction worker.

There was her answer about whether or not this was a setup.

Surrounded on all sides, nowhere to go, all she could think to do was pray. *Help, God.* And then she turned and faced the man who—while faceless—had haunted her sleeping and waking hours for the past ten years.

"Phil Winters." She shook her head. "But you're—"

"The mailman?" He laughed again. How was it possible that the sound seemed to grow more heavy with evil every time she heard it?

"No, that wasn't what I was going to say. You're nice, a good guy. You've talked to me before when I got the mail at my mailbox, from the time I was a little girl."

"Sure. You weren't an irritating kid and I had the time." He shrugged. "Now you're in the way of something I want. And you did something very, very bad."

"What?"

"You spoke up when you should have kept your mouth shut. You came forward and told the truth—for what reason I'll never know, because it's not like it benefitted you to get a bunch of my men arrested. You had to talk about what you were told not to, and you're the only one who has or will pay for it, Gemma Phillips. This is what you've chosen."

Before she could open her mouth to argue, the man standing behind her had pulled a dark sack over her face and she was being shoved into a vehicle—she'd guess Phil's.

Then they were driving. And she didn't know where. Didn't know where to tell Matt to find her. Didn't know how to get in touch with him anyway.

By the time she figured any of that out, there was a good possibility it would be too late.

Ignoring Gemma's calls was killing something inside him, but what else could he do? His job was gone because he'd gotten involved with the one woman in town who'd seen beyond his past and wanted a relationship with him. The only woman he'd ever wanted to spend all his time with, maybe think about growing old with.

And the only one who was 100 percent off-limits to him.

Matt ran the sander over the kayak's edge, slipped a little and almost turned the whole thing into firewood. It was too late in the process to be making holes in his work. If he did, there would literally be no way to fix it. These kinds of boats, the started-from-a-solid-log kayaks, had to stay whole from the beginning, be shaped with care, or they were essentially doomed.

He worked more cautiously, mind moving to

Gemma again. People weren't like these kayaks. People could get holes and God could fix them, rebuild them so they were better than they'd been before.

Maybe that was what drew them together. A knowledge that they'd each been broken by things in their past, but were almost put back together now. And maybe if both of them would stop fighting it in their own ways they'd be fully healed. Whole. Better than new.

They both needed to let the past go.

He turned the sander off, just stood there staring at the wood while his mind tried to wrestle with the thoughts developing.

It was true. He wasn't the same man he would have been if he'd had a nice childhood, had a dad who cared. But with God's help, maybe he was a better man than he would have been otherwise. Maybe the job didn't define him; maybe it didn't matter what the chief or the town or anyone else thought.

Maybe he should just accept God's grace in his own life and go out and live.

This time he set the sander down, reached for his phone, which had sat neglected on the workshop counter, and checked his missed calls. Five from Gemma this morning. He shook his head. Stupid pride had kept him from answering, but losing his job hadn't been her fault, and pulling away from her now wasn't going to get his job back. Instead, he was just drilling a hole in their relationship that would have to be mended later.

Thankfully he knew God could mend that, too. That was the beauty of grace—nothing was too far gone. He slid the phone in his pocket, felt to make sure he still had his keys on the carabiner on his belt loop and headed for his car. He was going to do better than call her; he was going to go see her, apologize in person.

He drove to the historical society office at the Hamilton Estate, ignored the fact that there was a patrol car parked where he felt he should have been and got out of the car and walked toward the door.

"She's not here," Ryan Townsend, the construction crew foreman called from where he sat on top of the museum's frame, hammering something. Matt liked how he wasn't just a figurehead, giving instructions while his men worked—he got right in there, too.

"Gemma?" Matt clarified, not having realized the construction workers had been paying that much attention to how much time they spent together.

Townsend nodded. "I heard someone got in a wreck here this morning, though. You could check and see if it was her car. It's already been towed, I guess. I just got here half an hour ago."

Matt glanced at his watch. Not even eleven o'clock. Unless the wreck had happened sometime before nine, he highly doubted the damaged car would be cleared already. He happened to know that Levi Meyer, who ran the only towing company in town, was taking the morning off to stay with his wife and their new baby girl, who had been born the day before.

Unless an out-of-town company had been called. But something in his gut made him doubt that today. "You have any guys who were here this morning who might have seen what happened?"

"A couple. Some of my guys are missing this morning, mostly the new hires."

"New hires?"

Ryan shrugged. "The historical society has got us on a pretty tight deadline, so there are guys I added to the crew just a little after the project began. So they've been here for a couple of weeks anyway, but they're not on my usual crew."

"And they're the ones missing?" Matt started toward the construction site, lengthening his stride. "I need to talk to someone who was here this morning."

There weren't many men working today,

something he hadn't noticed when he'd pulled in. "Any of you guys here this morning?" Ryan called.

The men shook their heads.

"Then, who was it who told me about the wreck here?" Ryan continued. "How did you find that out?"

"I heard about it in town," one of them spoke up. "Someone was talking about it down at the docks when I was finishing my morning coffee."

"So everyone working this morning has disappeared?"

"I guess so."

"And everyone working this morning was part of the new crew?"

Ryan scratched his head. "Come to think of it, yes. I would have been here with them, but my AC froze up at my house and I had to see about that before I could come."

"I was supposed to be here, too," someone else spoke up. "But I got a call this morning telling me that the materials I needed hadn't been delivered and not to bother coming in until closer to lunch. I thought it was you." He directed the last statement at Ryan. "But if it wasn't…"

"If it wasn't, then someone else engineered

it so that only the new construction workers were here." Matt clenched his fists.

"Jackson, you're in charge," Ryan yelled at one of the workman, then turned to Matt. "I can't believe this. What can I do?"

Matt almost told him nothing. This wasn't Ryan's problem—he wasn't an officer. But technically neither was Matt at the moment, and he wasn't going to sit here and do nothing while Gemma was possibly in danger. Maybe he was overreacting, all of this was coincidence and Gemma was home eating a pint of ice cream over their breakup. But that wasn't like Gemma. If anything, he'd guess that her breakup remedy meant focusing on work. If she wasn't here, then that meant something was wrong, and he wasn't going to rest until he'd found her.

The tightness in his chest led him to believe that that wouldn't be an easy task. Because somehow he knew the truth. Her stalker had her.

What he would do now was anyone's guess. Matt had to stop the killer before he hurt Gemma. Or worse.

SIXTEEN

The back of the mail truck smelled like hot cardboard, dust and metal. They'd snatched the sack off as soon as they'd tossed her into the truck, so apparently its only use had been to surprise her enough into inaction so they could tie her up and throw her in there.

Then they'd taken the sack off. Clearly they didn't care that she could identify them. In fact, it seemed as if they wanted her to *know* they were planning to kill her. Otherwise why go to the trouble of removing the bag?

But Gemma kept her eyes closed for the moment as the truck bumped down a back road on its way to who knew where. Denial? Did she think that maybe if she didn't open her eyes, they'd change their minds, let her go free?

Only there was no way that would happen. Not with Phil being determined enough to eliminate her from the picture in the first place.

"Why not just kill me now?" she yelled to

Phil, pretty sure he could hear her since the truck wasn't that big. "I know you're going to." Was she succeeding in making her voice sound brave? Strong? Gemma didn't know. But even if she couldn't control her circumstances, she could at least try to stay in control of herself.

Maybe that was all she had control over all along. Not over the situations she stumbled upon, the freakish incidents of being in the wrong place at the wrong time. But she did have a choice about how she reacted, how *she* viewed herself because of those things. Matt was right—it was easier to hold on to the past, to identify herself by it. But easy wasn't always right. And it was time for her to move on. She needed to define herself in a new way now.

Except...wasn't defining who she was on her own still missing the point?

How do You define me? She finally dared to ask God the question she'd always feared the answer to, here on the floor of a mail truck, smashed between boxes.

Bible verses scrolled through her head, like flipping through a three-by-five stack of memory verses she'd had in her growing-up years.

Loved. Safe. Known by name. His child. A woman who had gone through trials and come out stronger on the other side. Someone God was making brave. Someone who loved to find the best in others, find the best in ventures like the museum and show other people the positives of any situation.

By His grace Gemma was all of those things and whatever else He said she was. Not just "adopted," not the witness to a crime, not Claire's younger sister. To one degree or another, it was time to let those go.

Instead, she needed to see herself as Gemma Phillips. His.

The truck jerked to a stop. Gemma fought to keep control of her breathing.

At least she knew now. And with that knowledge…she wasn't going to die without a fight. If she was God's, if He saw her as the Gemma Phillips He'd made her to be, no matter what happened, then He might still have a purpose for her. And part of that purpose might even be her dreams: adding "wife"—*Matt's wife*—and eventually "mom" to her identity.

Please let me live, she prayed, heart finding the familiar whisper of words to God something that still felt right and natural even after all this time of silence between them.

Then the door of the truck opened. Phil was there again, face looking older, rougher than it had not long before.

"I'm sure you've already realized that once the police knew someone was after you, it was pointless to make things look like an accident. But I see no reason to make it too easy for them to find you. The more time and resources they devote to you, the less they'll have to focus on identifying me."

"So where are we?" The gravel road they'd been on had dead-ended into the woods. While the foliage was still familiar, and they hadn't been driving for long enough to be far from Treasure Point, the area wasn't familiar to her.

He raised his eyebrows, smiled slowly. "You don't know? Oh, good, that makes this better." He gave her a shove. "Walk this way."

Gemma could see a narrow path through the dense trees, which was evidently what her captor wanted her to take. She glanced back at him, wondering what her chances of escaping were if she just ran.

He patted his side, where she now noticed a lump on his hip. "Forty-five auto," he said, confirming that it was the outline of a gun that she saw.

So much for the thought of running.

She kept moving forward, deeper into the woods. Gemma still didn't recognize where they were, but she kept going.

Until the path reached a clearing and she caught sight of several other paths connecting to it in the distance. Those paths she recognized.

She looked at Phil. He widened his smile, showed every one of his crooked teeth. "Now you've got it." He nodded once, confirming her realization.

They were back where they had started ten years ago, deep in the woods where she'd heard his fight with Harris, where she'd managed to run away. Where Harris had died.

The eerie thought struck her as she looked down at the ground—if she could move the years of overgrowth and dirt, would there still be blood on this spot?

She shivered.

She wasn't going to let it end like this.

Options flashed through her mind, one by one like slides in a presentation. Matt? She'd try to call again if she could but Phil would notice if she pulled out her phone. And anyway, he wasn't talking to her, so she doubted he'd answer this time. Would he give their relationship another chance if she lived? Gemma hoped so. Thought he would.

Disarming Phil was a great option, but she didn't possess those kinds of skills. That option would get her shot the quickest.

She could wait and see…but hadn't she heard never to go with an abductor, not to cooperate? She'd already done that—a mistake, but one she'd seen no help for—and it didn't make sense to her to compound that mistake by staying passive.

That left running. The path to the construction site of the museum was the obvious choice, which was probably why Phil had positioned himself between her and that pathway.

What about...

Their beach—hers and Matt's—was only a quarter mile or so away. Hadn't he told her there was a kayak hidden there, too? Another place he'd used to store the boats that had let him escape his life with his dad.

She couldn't know for sure if the boat was usable. And she'd have to paddle through open ocean from here to the Hamilton Estate. Treasure Point itself was too far. So she'd still have to run through the woods, get the kayak, paddle away without getting shot and from there... would there be people she recognized at the construction site now, or just more of Phil's guys, ready to manhandle her into the back of another truck and then who knew where?

Gemma didn't know. But it was all she had.

As soon as he was distracted, she ran. Again. Feet pounding the same Georgia dirt they'd pounded against ten years ago when she'd run from this same man.

Except this time she was less afraid. This time she didn't wonder what would happen, didn't harbor the same level of anxiety. God had brought her through the past ten years right up until now, even when she hadn't believed He was watching over her, hadn't acknowledged that He cared about her anymore. So whatever happened now, He'd bring her through it. She knew now, from experience, that He gave strength. Grace. And, hopefully, speed.

Gemma didn't dare glance behind her as she ran, knowing it would only slow her down. Dirt flew up, leaves crunched under her and she pushed through the brush anywhere it had grown over the trail. She was pretty sure she'd have several scratches on her arms when this was done, but right now she wasn't taking the time to check. A little blood on her forearms was better than being dead.

And then she was there, safely at the beach and when she looked around, she was still alone. He hadn't followed her? She couldn't decide if that comforted or concerned her. If he wasn't following her, what was his plan?

It didn't matter right now. All that mattered was that she did the best she could to save herself.

She found the kayak tied to an old piece of driftwood at the edge of the beach. She untied it, thankful she'd found it, and then remembered. Paddle. She needed a paddle. Had Matt mentioned where he kept that?

Panicked, she looked around the kayak, didn't see it anywhere. Finally she glanced inside the boat itself. There it was, broken into two pieces for storage purposes. She snapped it together, dragged the boat down to the ocean.

God, please let this work.

And then she was out in the open water, the waves by the shore gently rocking her boat up and down. The water would only get more rough the farther out she went.

Gemma hoped she wasn't just moving from one type of certain death to another.

When both he and Ryan were in his truck—he'd had to turn in his patrol car when he'd been put on leave—Matt had immediately started for the dock. Whitetail Island had already served as the hiding place for two bodies; it seemed a likely location for whoever was behind this to stash one more. The thought made his stomach revolt. He would do anything he could to prevent Gemma from becoming another missing body. And one way or another, this was going to end today.

Matt just hoped it ended the way he wanted it to. With Gemma alive and willing to forgive him for being an idiot and ever even considering letting her go.

His truck practically flew down the road, kicking up dust and throwing rocks. Matt didn't care. He couldn't be too late to save Gemma.

Not that he didn't think she could take care of herself. She'd proved that she had a sharp mind, could pay attention to details, could get herself out of some scary situations.

But this was different. This was a face-to-face showdown with a man who wanted her dead. A man who'd already killed the three other people who had gotten in his way.

Matt swallowed hard, jammed his foot down a little harder on the gas, not easing up until their destination came into view.

"The docks?" Ryan asked.

"We need to head to Whitetail Island." It was just a hunch, but it was the best he had.

A patrol car pulled in beside him as soon as he'd opened the door. For a second, Matt thought his part in this was over. He was going to be forced to sit on the sidelines and wait to hear if Gemma was rescued or not.

But instead of the chief or Lieutenant Davies, both of whom probably would have benched him for good, it was Clay.

"Hey," he said in his easy way as he climbed out of his patrol car. "What are you doing over here? Not going back to Whitetail Island to investigate more, are you? Aren't you off the case?"

Off the case and maybe out of a job.

"Listen, Gemma's gone. The killer has her and I need to find her now."

"And you think they're at Whitetail?" Clay shook his head. "This area has been my patrol this morning, and I've kept a close eye on any boats, any activity out here at all. No one has gone that way."

"No one? You're sure?"

"Positive."

Only seconds passed before Matt climbed back into his truck. Clay was not only a co-worker, he was a friend, had been for a long time. Matt trusted him.

Clay knocked on Matt's window before Matt could put the truck in gear. He rolled it down.

"Where are you headed?"

"Back to the Hamilton Estate. We didn't see any evidence that they were still there, but there are trails in the woods. I guess we'll check those."

Clay nodded. "I'll follow you." He turned to his truck, paused, then turned back around. "There's also another place those trails connect to, farther down the road. Have you been down there?"

Matt had forgotten about it. But he nodded now, remembering going that way with buddies once or twice when they went hunting on someone else's land near there as high schoolers. "I think I know where you mean. You lead."

"See you there." And Clay was back in his car driving away, Matt and Ryan following close on his tail.

The dirt road past the Hamilton Estate was at least as dusty as the road to town, and since he was following another car now, visibility was even worse for Matt. He fought to keep his eyes on the road while keeping his speed up as high as he dared.

The road ended in a small clearing, nothing remarkable or memorable. Matt threw the truck into Park, opened his door and ran to the edge of the woods. "This way, right?" He turned to confirm with Clay, already set to take off when he got confirmation.

"Stop." Clay shook his head. "We can't just run in there."

"Why? He's got her, we don't. So we go." Even as he said it, Matt knew it didn't follow standard operating procedure, something he'd always done his best to follow down to the letter in his desperation to win approval. Right now none of that mattered, though. If what he was doing now was the last nail in the coffin of his career and saved Gemma? It would be worth it. Anything would be worth it.

Because he loved her.

"Let's get a plan together. You're thinking with your heart, man, but we've got to use our heads, too."

Matt nodded, eyes still focused on the paths through the woods that he believed would lead him to Gemma. "All right. Two minutes. You lay out a plan because you can think straight. And then we're going in."

Please don't let two minutes be too long.

The waves tossed Gemma with more force than she'd expected. Salty spray hit her in the face as she struggled to jam the paddle back into the water, push herself forward one more time. The wind tossed her hair around, long dark strands of it sometimes obscuring her vision. Surely it couldn't be far now. She squinted at the shoreline. Almost there. The Hamilton Estate had a little dock on a corner of land closest to the house, and that was where she was aiming.

God, please help.

It was all the prayer she could articulate, but her spirit meant it with everything within her, and her trust in God to hear her filled her with something that felt a lot like faith, like the faith she'd had before everything happened.

"Thank You." She whispered that one because He *had* helped her already. If nothing else, He'd helped her find her way back to Him, and there on the stormy gray-green ocean waves, something inside her finally felt at peace.

Whole.

Gemma paddled harder, determination growing with every stroke. She did the best she could to ignore the pain in her still-broken wrist, wishing she didn't have that working against her. Kayaking had been her only chance to stay alive—still was—and she wasn't going down without a fight. The dock grew larger in her vision and she aimed her kayak straight for it. The current ran this way and even though she had to fight with the waves now, it would be even more of a challenge to try to get back to the dock if she missed it. She had one shot at this. If it didn't work, she'd have to abandon this plan and try to kayak all the way into Treasure Point through marsh grass that would block her view.

This was it. She had to do it. Hands grasping the paddle tightly, she pushed one more time. Got it. The boat hit the dock and she reached with her hands, holding on to the old wood planks for dear life. A wave hit, slamming her into the dock and capsizing the kayak. Then it was gone, pulled back out when the waves went, and Gemma scrambled up onto the dock, dripping wet, but still alive.

For now.

She crept into the woods, doing her best to be as quiet as possible. From here, she'd need to turn right onto a narrow game trail that paralleled the shore, then work her way back left toward the—

"Hello, Gemma."

Hard steel jammed between her shoulder blades. She almost couldn't swallow. Couldn't breathe.

How had Phil gotten behind her? And how had he known where she'd be?

He chuckled. She hated it, wished she could plug her ears, make it go away—the worst sound she'd ever heard. "Did you really think you could climb into a boat like some kind of adventurer and somehow get away from what you deserve? It was logical to wait for you here—where else could you have gone? You broke your word, Gemma. And you have to pay."

"Broke my word?"

"Yes, I let you live a decade ago because

I thought it was understood that you would keep quiet. When you never gave the police my name, I thought you'd agreed."

"But I didn't."

He jammed the gun tighter. "Arguing? Aren't you supposed to beg for mercy at this point?" More laughter. "That's what everyone else has done. All four of them so far."

"Four?"

"That's right. Four. No one will ever link me to that fourth. Now." He used the gun to push her forward a foot or two. "I'm going to bury you right here, so you may as well be close. You've caused me enough trouble. Which is why I'm looking forward to killing you more than any of the o—" A gunshot cut him off.

Gemma closed her eyes, waited for the pain, for the nothingness.

Instead, the pressure on her back eased and Phil crumpled to the ground. She swung around and looked at his body. Dead.

Gemma looked up. Friend or foe? After walking up on the argument between gang members last time, she knew that fights within a crime ring could turn deadly. Yes, the shooter wanted Phil dead, but that didn't mean he wanted Gemma to stay alive. She wasn't going to calm down until she knew it was a law enforcement officer who was her rescuer. Movement caught the corner of her eye, maybe fifty yards away. Not an officer, at least not one in uniform.

Michael O'Dell.

Matt's father.

SEVENTEEN

Matt, Clay and Ryan had been moving through the woods slowly until they heard the shot.

Then they ran. Clay was in front at first, and Matt tried to overtake him, determined to find her first but before he caught up, a guy he didn't recognize wearing a construction outfit appeared out of nowhere and pulled a weapon from the waist of his pants. Leveled it at Clay.

"No!" Matt shot and the man fell.

Matt glanced at him, indecision making him almost useless. He had to get to Gemma.

"I've got him. You go get her." Clay already had his handcuffs off his belt, was moving toward the suspect.

Matt nodded and took off running again, hearing the footsteps behind him that said Ryan was right on his heels. The two of them were close to the end of the trail, approaching the clearing where Gemma had first stumbled upon the crime ring hiding their loot.

The first he noticed—even from far away—was blood, pooled on the ground underneath what looked like a human body. And his whole world stopped. Matt had thought things were bad when his mom left and he realized she wasn't coming back. Had thought the way his dad loved alcohol more than his son was bad enough. But the realization that he was looking at what had to be Gemma's body was worse than any of those, worse than both of them together.

More than he could take.

Anger felt like fire building in his veins and he ran closer, ready to find the man who had done this when he realized…it wasn't Gemma's body.

The body belonged to a man. One more glance at the gruesome sight confirmed the body was wearing a postal uniform. Phil? Phil Winters? It almost couldn't compute in Matt's brain that the older man had been the one who'd so desperately wanted Gemma dead.

"That's the guy?" Ryan asked. Matt then heard him throw up somewhere behind them. "Sorry, I'm not used to stuff like this."

"Don't apologize. No one should have to be." Sometimes Matt wondered if citizens realized how much police officers gave up to do the job they did, wondered if anyone ever appreciated the hate and hurt and gore they absorbed every day so the general public wouldn't have to. He looked around the area, and his eyes landed on the last man he'd ever expected to see again.

"Dad."

And it was as if someone had taken the world, turned it upside down and shaken it. And Matt wasn't even sure yet if the world would ever right itself, stop spinning. Because there was his dad.

And then Matt noticed the gun. "I need an explanation."

His dad pointed. "She's down there, on the beach somewhere. You should find her before she tries to escape and hurts herself. I tried to tell her I wouldn't hurt her..."

But she hadn't believed him. Matt didn't blame her. He still wasn't sure he believed it, either.

"Come with me," Matt ordered. "Leave the weapon here."

He nodded, followed Matt as he'd been asked to do.

Matt made his way down to the beach, visually scanned it until he noticed footprints in the sand, places where it looked kicked up. The trail led under the dock.

"Sit down," he told his dad. "Watch him." Those words were directed to Ryan.

"Matt?" The soft voice from underneath the old dock was the most beautiful one he'd ever heard.

"Gemma. You're alive. You're alive and I'm an idiot for ever letting you go, for not telling you how I've felt about you ever since high school PE class."

"Your dad. He shot him."

"Shot Phil?"

He'd made his way to the front of the dock now, and he could see Gemma underneath it, way in the back. He held out a hand and she crawled out. "Yes. He shot him and I didn't know for sure if he was really on our side or if he'd be after me, too, but there was nowhere to run anymore. So I stopped running. I hid and I prayed." She looked up at him, gave the smallest hint of a smile. "And you came."

He squeezed her hand. "I'm sorry for what I said, for how I left the other day."

"I needed to hear it. You were right, Matt. But that's in the past, just like everything else. Let's try to move on."

Matt lifted her face to his, locked his eyes with hers to make sure she'd hear his next words. "I'd love to move on if it's with you. I love you, Gemma Phillips."

"I love you, too."

* * *

Gemma couldn't believe how quickly crowds of law enforcement descended on what had been a desolate spot in the woods. Some came, she gathered from hearing conversations, to take away the construction worker who worked for Phil and had been shot. According to that man, who'd been happy to give them all the details the police wanted about the crimes he'd committed when he heard it might lessen his sentence, there were three other construction workers who'd been on Phil's payroll. The chief dispatched several officers to round them up, but didn't seem too worried about catching them.

"You're sure you're okay?" Gemma's dad had gotten to the scene right away.

"I'm fine, Daddy." Gemma glanced over at Matt, who stood near his own dad, watching him be handcuffed for the second time in Matt's life. Matt said something to his dad, brushed at his own cheek and then walked her way.

"What will happen to him? He saved my life."

Matt nodded. "I know. Everyone else knows now." He shrugged his shoulders. "I don't know what will happen to him. But I think I'll go visit this time. He…he did a lot of things wrong…" Matt reached for Gemma's hand and squeezed it. "But if he really broke out of jail for the reasons he says—because he heard about Phil stalking you and wanted to stop him—then maybe he's done something right, too."

"He could have made things a lot easier on everyone by just telling the authorities about Phil. But I suppose he had his reasons for keeping quiet on that point. And given the lengths he went to, to make things right, he should get a lesser sentence," Gemma's dad agreed. "Also, Matt…we were wrong about you, Gemma's mom and I. I want you to know we are sorry for the way we treated you when you were a guest in our house." He smiled at Gemma. "Our daughter is special to us. We may be a bit over-protective. But we look forward to getting to know more about who *you* are. Not who your family is, although as you said, there may even be some good there, too."

Matt nodded. "Thank you, sir."

Gemma was sure if her smile tried to widen any farther it would get stuck that way. She held his hand a little tighter.

"Young lady." Gemma hadn't heard the chief approaching, but here he was behind her. "You are one of the bravest people I've ever met. And I don't know what happened ten years ago, which of our officers dropped the ball and didn't believe your recollections of the crime were all accurate, but I want to apologize on their behalf. A murderer could have continued to go free if it wasn't for you coming home and being willing to help us bring him to justice." The chief glanced in Matt's direction. "I know you were a part of some of the investigating, informally, while Matt was protecting you. And I appreciate what you did. I appreciate what *both* of you did, and while it was a bit…unorthodox for the two of you to be as close as you were while being involved in a case together, I think in the end everything worked out." He turned to Matt. "Go out tonight, celebrate. But I expect to see you in my office first thing tomorrow morning to wrap this thing up. This is your case, O'Dell. Probably always should have been. And I'd be proud to have you finish working it."

Matt nodded. Gemma thought he might have stood a little taller. "Thank you, sir. I'll be there."

She smiled up at him.

They stayed in the woods for another hour, giving statements and retelling the events of the day as best they could remember them. Finally, they were both cleared to leave.

"Want to come to my house for dinner?" Matt asked. "I called when I had a minute earlier and invited a couple of people who I thought would want to come, too."

Gemma nodded. Celebrating with friends sounded perfect. It did good things to her heart to realize there were people who wanted to celebrate with both of them. Together. Here in this crazy little town where both of them had once been defined by mistakes that hadn't been theirs. "I'd love to."

He swung her by Claire's house, and Gemma ran inside and changed into a turquoise sundress. Maybe a bit overdressed for a backyard cookout, but she wanted to look good, mostly because she *felt* good. Felt free.

Felt as if she could finally be the Gemma Phillips she'd always wanted to be. The one God wanted her to be, with His help.

Matt's appreciative gaze when she climbed back into the truck made dressing up worth it.

The drive to his house didn't take long, and when they got there several people were already milling around. She recognized Adam Cole, the pastor of one of the churches in Treasure Point who was also Shiloh's husband, at the grill. There were her parents talking to Mary Hamilton—who Gemma still needed to talk to about the museum. There was Claire. A few officers she'd recognized as Matt's friends, including Clay Hitchcock.

"I'll be right back. I'm going to run in and change." Matt grinned. "Don't go anywhere."

She didn't, just grabbed a can of Coke and started mingling. She was overwhelmed at the number of people who had come to share their excitement over solving the case. Even Cindy Anne was there—the first Gemma had seen of her since that awful interview—and she gave Gemma a small smile and made a comment about her doing a good job at the museum that could *almost* be considered an apology. At least, it was probably the closest Cindy Anne would ever get to issuing one.

After a short time, she caught sight of Matt walking out of his front door. As he walked toward her, everything got a little quiet. And everyone looked at him.

Then at Gemma. Expectantly. And her breath caught a little in her throat, for once in a good way, as she wondered if she was right about what was going to happen next...

He walked onto the porch, then down the steps and straight to Gemma, the grin on his face widening with every step he took. In the time it took for him to move closer, she looked him over. His hair was wet, as though he'd taken a quick shower, and he was wearing khakis with a blue shirt that made his eyes look even more full of life than they ever had—or maybe finishing this case had done that.

Then again, maybe God had done it. He'd

certainly made Gemma feel lighter—more free than she ever could remember feeling before.

"Gemma Phillips." He focused his smile on her, lowered himself to one knee.

And then her breath wasn't catching anymore because now she was holding her breath entirely, afraid if she moved at all, she'd ruin this moment, realize it was a dream or something. Only it wasn't, it was real and it was happening. To her. To *them.*

"I've thought you were the most special woman I've ever known for at least the past decade, and for the past few weeks you've proved that to be true. You're brave, you're strong and just like you're the woman I want by my side for the rest of my life, I want to be the man by your side for the rest of yours. Will you marry me, Gemma?"

She nodded, broke into a grin. "Yes. Yes, Matt, I would love to."

He slid the ring on her finger—a gorgeous diamond in a vintage-inspired setting, classic Southern style. She watched as he did that, then as soon as it was on, he stood. She lifted her face to his.

And their lips met in a long, slow kiss.

* * * * *

Dear Reader,

I loved being back in Treasure Point for this book and I hope you did, too! There's something about the southern Georgia coastline, with the way the ocean breeze whispers through the Spanish moss, that has always felt both comforting and mysterious to me. That's why it's one of my favorite places to set a book. I wish Treasure Point were a real place so that I could visit—and you could, too!—but if you get to spend time in Darien or Savannah, Georgia, I think you'll find that they are pretty similar.

When I finished my first book, *Treasure Point Secrets*, I knew that Matt O'Dell would need his own happily-ever-after. It took some time to figure out what the perfect woman for him would be like, but once Gemma developed as a character, I loved the way their relationship played out. Matt and Gemma's story is one that has been in my mind for a long time, but because of some difficult seasons in my own life, it has taken longer than usual to get it on paper and into your hands. Thank you, Reader, for reading it, and for letting me tell you this story.

God teaches me things through the stories I write, and I have to say that I learned a lot while I was writing this book. Like Gemma, I learned to look toward the future instead of letting the past define me, and I also learned a lot about God's grace. While I hope that the story has entertained you and provided a fun break from laundry, dishes or whatever your "real life" looks like, I also hope that you learned something through it, and that maybe God will use it to draw you closer to Him.

I love hearing from readers, and I'd love to hear from you! You can get in touch with me through email, sarahvarland@gmail.com, or find me on my personal blog:

espressoinalatteworld.blogspot.com.

Sarah Varland

LARGER-PRINT BOOKS!

GET 2 FREE LARGER-PRINT NOVELS PLUS 2 FREE MYSTERY GIFTS

Love Inspired®

Larger-print novels are now available...

YES! Please send me 2 FREE LARGER-PRINT Love Inspired® novels and my 2 FREE mystery gifts (gifts are worth about $10). After receiving them, if I don't wish to receive any more books, I can return the shipping statement marked "cancel." If I don't cancel, I will receive 6 brand-new novels every month and be billed just $5.49 per book in the U.S. or $5.99 per book in Canada. That's a savings of at least 19% off the cover price. It's quite a bargain! Shipping and handling is just 50¢ per book in the U.S. and 75¢ per book in Canada.* I understand that accepting the 2 free books and gifts places me under no obligation to buy anything. I can always return a shipment and cancel at any time. Even if I never buy another book, the two free books and gifts are mine to keep forever.

122/322 IDN GH6D

Name	(PLEASE PRINT)	
Address		Apt. #
City	State/Prov.	Zip/Postal Code

Signature (if under 18, a parent or guardian must sign)

Mail to the **Reader Service:**
IN U.S.A.: P.O. Box 1867, Buffalo, NY 14240-1867
IN CANADA: P.O. Box 609, Fort Erie, Ontario L2A 5X3

**Are you a current subscriber to Love Inspired® books and want to receive the larger-print edition?
Call 1-800-873-8635 or visit www.ReaderService.com.**

* Terms and prices subject to change without notice. Prices do not include applicable taxes. Sales tax applicable in N.Y. Canadian residents will be charged applicable taxes. Offer not valid in Quebec. This offer is limited to one order per household. Not valid to current subscribers to Love Inspired Larger-Print books. All orders subject to credit approval. Credit or debit balances in a customer's account(s) may be offset by any other outstanding balance owed by or to the customer. Please allow 4 to 6 weeks for delivery. Offer available while quantities last.

LILP15

REQUEST YOUR FREE BOOKS!
2 FREE WHOLESOME ROMANCE NOVELS
IN LARGER PRINT
PLUS 2
FREE
MYSTERY GIFTS

☆☆☆☆☆☆☆☆☆☆☆☆☆☆☆☆☆☆☆☆☆

HEARTWARMING™

☆☆☆☆☆☆☆☆☆☆☆☆☆☆☆☆☆☆☆☆☆

Wholesome, tender romances

YES! Please send me 2 FREE Harlequin® Heartwarming Larger-Print novels and my 2 FREE mystery gifts (gifts worth about $10). After receiving them, if I don't wish to receive any more books, I can return the shipping statement marked "cancel." If I don't cancel, I will receive 4 brand-new larger-print novels every month and be billed just $5.24 per book in the U.S. or $5.99 per book in Canada. That's a savings of at least 19% off the cover price. It's quite a bargain! Shipping and handling is just 50¢ per book in the U.S. and 75¢ per book in Canada.* I understand that accepting the 2 free books and gifts places me under no obligation to buy anything. I can always return a shipment and cancel at any time. Even if I never buy another book, the two free books and gifts are mine to keep forever.

161/361 IDN GHX2

Name   (PLEASE PRINT)

Address   Apt. #

City   State/Prov.   Zip/Postal Code

Signature (if under 18, a parent or guardian must sign)

Mail to the **Reader Service:**
IN U.S.A.: P.O. Box 1867, Buffalo, NY 14240-1867
IN CANADA: P.O. Box 609, Fort Erie, Ontario L2A 5X3

* Terms and prices subject to change without notice. Prices do not include applicable taxes. Sales tax applicable in N.Y. Canadian residents will be charged applicable taxes. Offer not valid in Quebec. This offer is limited to one order per household. Not valid for current subscribers to Harlequin Heartwarming larger-print books. All orders subject to credit approval. Credit or debit balances in a customer's account(s) may be offset by any other outstanding balance owed by or to the customer. Please allow 4 to 6 weeks for delivery. Offer available while quantities last.

Your Privacy—The Reader Service is committed to protecting your privacy. Our Privacy Policy is available online at www.ReaderService.com or upon request from the Reader Service.

We make a portion of our mailing list available to reputable third parties that offer products we believe may interest you. If you prefer that we not exchange your name with third parties, or if you wish to clarify or modify your communication preferences, please visit us at www.ReaderService.com/consumerchoice or write to us at Reader Service Preference Service, P.O. Box 9062, Buffalo, NY 14240-9062. Include your complete name and address.

WESTERN WP PROMISES

YES! Please send me **The Western Promises Collection** in Larger Print. This collection begins with 3 FREE books and 2 FREE gifts (gifts valued at approx. $14.00 retail) in the first shipment, along with the other first 4 books from the collection! If I do not cancel, I will receive 8 monthly shipments until I have the entire 51-book Western Promises collection. I will receive 2 or 3 FREE books in each shipment and I will pay just $4.99 US/ $5.89 CDN for each of the other four books in each shipment, plus $2.99 for shipping and handling per shipment. *If I decide to keep the entire collection, I'll have paid for only 32 books, because 19 books are FREE! I understand that accepting the 3 free books and gifts places me under no obligation to buy anything. I can always return a shipment and cancel at any time. My free books and gifts are mine to keep no matter what I decide.

272 HCN 3070 472 HCN 3070

Name	(PLEASE PRINT)	
Address		Apt. #
City	State/Prov.	Zip/Postal Code

Signature (if under 18, a parent or guardian must sign)

Mail to the **Reader Service:**
IN U.S.A.: P.O. Box 1867, Buffalo, NY 14240-1867
IN CANADA: P.O. Box 609, Fort Erie, Ontario L2A 5X3

* Terms and prices subject to change without notice. Prices do not include applicable taxes. Sales tax applicable in N.Y. Canadian residents will be charged applicable taxes. This offer is limited to one order per household. All orders subject to approval. Credit or debit balances in a customer's account(s) may be offset by any other outstanding balance owed by or to the customer. Please allow 4 to 6 weeks for delivery. Offer available while quantities last. Offer not available to Quebec residents.

Your Privacy—The Reader Service is committed to protecting your privacy. Our Privacy Policy is available online at www.ReaderService.com or upon request from the Reader Service.

We make a portion of our mailing list available to reputable third parties that offer products we believe may interest you. If you prefer that we not exchange your name with third parties, or if you wish to clarify or modify your communication preferences, please visit us at www.ReaderService.com/consumerschoice or write to us at Reader Service Preference Service, P.O. Box 9062, Buffalo, NY 14240-9062. Include your complete name and address.

WPBPA16R

READERSERVICE.COM

Manage your account online!

- Review your order history
- Manage your payments
- Update your address

We've designed the Reader Service website just for you.

Enjoy all the features!

- Discover new series available to you, and read excerpts from any series.
- Respond to mailings and special monthly offers.
- Connect with favorite authors at the blog.
- Browse the Bonus Bucks catalog and online-only exculsives.
- Share your feedback.

Visit us at:

ReaderService.com